BAD GIRL

WICKED #2

PIPER LAWSON

Line and copy editing by Cassie Roberston
Cover by Natasha Snow
Cover photography by Lindee Robinson

1

HALEY

For four hours on the bus to Atlanta, my earbuds plugged in and some new indie act providing a subtle soundtrack to the passing scenery, my brain's been going full-tilt. The would've waltz, the should've samba, and the could've cha-cha.

Maybe I shouldn't have run on my birthday.

Maybe Jax had a good reason for not telling me about Cross.

Maybe I should've texted him, called him, something.

I give myself until the bus pulls into the station to indulge my doubts. Then I cut it off.

Tonight's about reminding myself I did the right thing, not rehashing every decision I've made in my life like a washing machine on spin cycle.

I leave my bags in a locker at the bus depot and take my backpack with me to the venue. Find my seat near the back in the electric darkness.

Around me, people talk, drink, and gossip. Some of it's about Jax. It feels as if they're talking about a friend behind his back.

Somewhere in the midst of the opening act, I notice the buzzing. Not around me, but inside me. As though something's trying to get out.

When the changeover happens, it intensifies.

After two months bartending in Nashville, my feet are calloused from the heels, my hand-eye coordination's improved tenfold, and I'm tanned from spending my few days off outside with Lita.

I'm more exposed, but I'm tougher too.

Or so I thought.

Now, I realize I'm wrong. I shouldn't be here.

I push my way out of the row until I make it to the aisle. But before I can get to the exit door, the place comes down.

The opening line of one of Jax's classic hits

splits the screaming, uttered in a voice that haunts my dreams.

I can't stop myself from turning.

The black button-down with short sleeves shows off his tattoos. Faded jeans I think I've touched worship his long, hard legs. He's a hundred feet away, but I can smell him. My fingers itch for the feeling of his body through the thin T-shirt.

If there ever was a man who looked like he was fucking a microphone on stage, it's Jax. Not because he's overtly sexual, but because Jax Jamieson is *vital*.

It's the first word that comes to mind when I see him because he's like life itself. So real it hurts.

His hair falls across his face, and I'd swear my eyes lock with his.

Of course when you're onstage, you can't see anything through the lights. But there are techniques to make it feel as though you're connecting with the audience, and Jax works them all.

If I wanted closure, there's no way in hell I'm getting it tonight.

He's on fire. This is his third-to-last show, and

he's selling it, every second, as though he already misses the stage.

For that moment, I'm just a fan.

And I hate that he's leaving.

After the show, the energy dissipates, a slow leak like the crowd pouring out the venue doors.

I stay behind. My gaze finds the sound booth. The sight of the man there, stooped and gray, warms me.

Until I see him reaching for an unfamiliar piece of equipment and hefting it in his arms.

I make my way toward the booth, tripping past the last of the escaping fans in my hurry. "Jerry! Put that down."

He sets down the piece of digital equipment with a thud and straightens. "Miss Telfer." He smiles. "Help me with this, will you? I need to get it out to the truck."

For a moment, I wonder if he's even realized I haven't been on tour.

"Why don't you call Nina to send someone?" I look down toward the stage. The band is long gone, but the crew is packing up.

"No!" The sharpness of his tone startles me. "This is my new toy. I won't let those animals put their hands on it. Take it to the truck for me?"

I hold in my sigh. I should be on my way back to the bus station to take the overnight home, but the look on Jerry's face has me caving. I loop the cords over my arm and lift the box. Thanks to bartending, I'm stronger than I was.

"Where's your new helper?" I ask as he walks toward the stage door with me.

"I told Nina I didn't need one."

My eyes widen. "You didn't."

"I had you. And now I have your program." He says it with pride. "I'm better than new."

Guilt creeps in as Jerry waves at the security guard to let him know that I'm with him.

The exterior door opens, and I'm deafened.

There are fans. Not dozens, but hundreds. Maybe thousands.

Security's trying to keep it under control, but they and the barricade seem to be fighting a losing battle.

I pick my way toward the truck, trying not to trip though I can't see my feet.

I drift too close to the roped-off mob, and there's tugging on Jerry's equipment.

Dammit.

I wrestle it back.

Some girl manages to shove over one of the posts holding up the rope, and another lunges over the barricade.

It's a stampede as one after another flows through the lowered barrier.

A phone hits me. Next, a cardboard cutout of Jax scratches the side of my face. I can't block them because my hands are full, but I tilt and fall, clutching Jerry's damned toy to keep it safe.

Something sharp hits me on the head, and my mouth falls open in shock.

Numbness washes over me as if I'm on a boat being gently rocked by the waves.

Until I feel hands clamp around my arms.

Don't fucking touch me. I want to scream it, but I can't.

My stomach rolls. "Let go," I moan instead.

The grip gets tighter, and it feels like coils binding my skin. Ropes burning as I twist and try to escape.

The screaming gets louder. I'm lifted into someone's arms.

Hands are everywhere.

I fight them, or try to, until a familiar voice makes me give in.

"Shut up, Hales."

Those muttered words, too close to my ear, are the last thing I hear before the world goes black.

2

"Is she bleeding?"

"You need to splint it."

"How the hell do you know?"

"I won *Doctor Who: The Adventure Games* in like six days."

"That's a video game, asshole. And also not a real doctor."

I ignore Kyle and Brick bickering behind me.

The towel I grabbed has stage tape on one end, and I rip it off as I run the thing under cold water.

Drip marks stain the floor as I return to the dressing room, step over the coffee table, and crouch in front of the figure in the armchair.

Her chin's almost on her skinned knees, her

arms looped around legs under a jean skirt I had to adjust when I set her down. The Converse sneakers haven't changed.

I brush the hair from Haley's face and press the towel to the scratch on her forehead as she hisses.

"Serves you right," I murmur. "Next time, leave crowd-surfing to the professionals."

"Never seen your firefighter routine, Jax." This from Brick, but I don't rise to the bait. "It's going to be all over the internet tomorrow."

Haley blinks, her lashes revealing brown eyes with green flecks. "Really?"

"Both of you are," Mace weighs in from where he's leaning against the wall in the corner. "What's with the cameo?"

"I heard this was the last chance to see Riot Act live." Her ankles cross in front of her as she leans back, shifting to get more comfortable as her eyes open for a moment only to drift closed again. "Had to come and get my chest signed."

Brick chuckles behind me, and Kyle sprints across the room. "I'll get a Sharpie."

I lean in to check the towel—there's hardly any blood on it, but I find a clean spot and press it back to her head.

"Already signed your chest," I murmur, low enough only she can hear.

Her shoulders twitch. The only sign she's heard me, but it's enough. My gaze lingers on the bare skin of her shoulders, and I have the random urge to cover her up.

Especially when Kyle appears at my side, bending over.

"What the hell are you doing?" I demand.

"The woman wants an autograph. Who am I to deny her?"

I turn toward him, and the look on my face has him lifting his hands in surrender. "I'll just leave this here." Kyle caps the pen and sets it on the table behind me.

"You staying away from the diner lobster, Mace?" Haley asks, looking past my shoulder.

"Try to stick to diner crab," he replies easily.

My mouth twitches, but it's not my guitarist I'm looking at. It's her.

I'm being studied by big hazel eyes framed in dark lashes, and I wish we were alone right now.

I don't know what I'd do with her. Strangle her, maybe. Kiss her, definitely.

From the look on her face, like she's overwhelmed, maybe she wants that too.

Or maybe she just hit her head.

"So Riot Act's announced their retirement," Haley says, breaking the silence. "I'm surprised no one's chained themselves to your tour bus."

"Madame Tussaud wrote to see if I could sit for my wax statue," I tell her.

She laughs, and I want to ask a million things.

How she is. If she's still pissed at me.

Whether she kept my hoodie.

It's the least appropriate thought right now, especially since I don't need a reminder of the time I yanked it off her. When I'd channeled every ounce of frustration into kissing her, swallowing her gasps as my tongue wrecked havoc with hers.

"What's that?" she asks, pointing to the braided bracelet on my wrist.

"Grace's kid made it," Mace says, dropping onto the sofa behind me.

"Annie?" Haley looks between us.

Before I can tell him to shut up, he plows on. "The night you left, she called to say her mom was missing. He flew to Dallas to find her."

Haley's expression fills with alarm. She shifts

forward, wringing the towel in her hands. "What happened? Is she okay? Is Annie—"

"Grace'd checked into the hospital." The look on her face tells me she understands why. "But they're going to be fine now. They're at the hotel. They're finishing up the tour with me."

"So, she left her husband." Her voice is hollow with shock.

I nod, picturing my sister's battered body in the hospital bed. The anger and resentment that fill my gut are the kind that never really leave.

"I wish you'd told me."

It's intimate, what she says and how she says it.

Kyle catches my eye from where he's packing his bag near the door.

I scratch at my chin because I'm still in stage makeup. I force myself not to let on how much her low voice affects me. "You were a tech on my tour for a month. We're ships passing."

If it sounds callous, it's not. It's reality.

Haley and I don't have a future.

We don't even have a past.

All we have is a stolen kiss and the kind of fragile trust that's made to be broken. By me, by her, by the world, until there's less than nothing left.

"I'm going to take this out to the bus," Mace says, shifting off the couch. I don't look to see what he's talking about.

"Kyle, you wanna come with?"

"I want to hear about Haley's summer."

I close my eyes because I'm really ready to shove my band out the door and slam it in their faces right now. At least Mace knows it.

"Kyle? I'll let you show me how to make a Patreon donation for that wildlife artist."

"For real? Let's do it."

Then they're gone and it's just the two of us.

Somehow it feels like there's more space between us rather than less.

Haley breaks the silence first. "If we're passing ships, what's with the dramatic rescue? I'm not on your tour anymore. You don't owe me anything."

"I don't like seeing you get hurt."

Her eyes darken. "Then why didn't you tell me about Cross?"

I wonder if she's turned it over in her head as many times as I have the last two months.

I stare back at her. "I don't like seeing you get hurt," I repeat.

Since I made the deal with Cross to protect her, he's been silent.

Still... just because Haley and I won't be sleeping down the hall from one another doesn't mean I can't keep an eye on her.

She looks good despite the bump on the head that I'm pretty sure will resolve. Her sharp eyes still make me want to know what's going on behind them. The curves under her clothes are still seriously distracting. Her full lips have me wanting to see her smile or laugh or...

"School must be starting soon," I say, breaking the stillness. "You're going back to Philly?"

"Tonight." She glances up at the clock on the wall behind me. "I should probably get going." She makes no move to rise, just huffs out a little breath as she looks at me.

She's changed since she left. She's grown up. Where she would spill everything at my feet before, she's not going to now.

Endings suck no matter how you slice them. Our first was bad enough. It seems cruel to have another.

But life's cruel.

"Say something, Hales." I murmur it under my breath.

Her mouth twitches at the corner. "What kind of something."

"Anything. Let me in your head."

"Okay." Her cheeks flush, and that hint of embarrassment has me leaning in. "I had a dream you came after me. You walked in the door of the honky-tonk where I was working, and you told me you'd fucked up and you were sorry." She frowns. "And then you took the stage next to Prince and played the ukulele. That's when I should've known it was a dream."

A chuckle escapes. "You should've known it was a dream because no one just walks in the door at the Rockabilly. There's a line a mile long."

"You've been there?" Her eyes widen.

"Marty's place. She stocks some good bourbon."

"And Andre's. They got married."

"Huh." Sharing people in common makes it feel like we haven't spent the last two months apart.

It's all pretend. Because she's going back to her life and I'm—finally—going back to mine.

I don't know what to do here.

Because I don't, I stand.

She rises too.

And if that's not the perfect metaphor for how we are, I don't know what is.

This girl's my shadow. We're bound together by a thread that won't let go even though we're opposites in so many ways—she's bright, I'm dark; she's new, I'm jaded; she's curious, I'm closed off.

But from the second I noticed her, I can't unsee her.

"Haley."

We both turn to see Nina standing at the door, a knowing look on her face.

"I heard you made an impression on the crowd. Or they made one on you." Her face tightens with concern. "You okay?"

"Good as new. And I promise I'm not suing anyone."

"Good girl. Let me walk you out."

I shake my head. "I can do it."

Nina holds up her hands. "Jax? You go out

there again and there's going to be an actual riot."

I wonder if that's the real reason or if Nina wants to keep us apart.

Regardless, Haley steps forward first. "Well, it was a hell of a show."

"Best ever?" I study her face.

Her expression shifts. "Yeah. Best ever." She swallows. "Goodbye, Jax."

"See you, Hales."

Before I can react, Haley closes the distance between us. Her arms wind around my neck.

Her scent washes over me, and I close my eyes. I've done two gigs in Hawaii, and I swear she smells like the air there.

I can feel Nina's gaze on us.

Fuck Nina.

I wrap my arms around Haley's waist, pulling her harder against me even though I shouldn't.

"So, you knew where I was, but you never thought about coming to check it out, huh?" she murmurs against my neck, low enough only I can hear. Her voice is a tease, stroking down my spine.

"If I'd chased your ass down"—her hair

tickles my lips, and I bury my nose in her—"I wouldn't have come back."

I'm the one to step back first. When I do, I see a wry smile pulling at her mouth.

That's good.

Because it's better if we both think I'm joking.

Getting into my apartment takes longer than usual. The key turns in the lock, but as I lean against the door, it won't open.

I shove, and something gives.

"Roomie!" Serena's voice sounds far away. "It's about time."

I glance at the chair that'd been blocking the way. "You barricaded yourself in here?"

"Not me. Scrunchie. He's been exercising a lot of independence lately. The door's open for even a minute, and he slips out."

My roommate, dressed in a crop top and skinny jeans that show off her naturally flat stomach, crosses to the black-and-white mop in the middle of the living room floor. "I took him to the dog park the other day, and everyone looked at me like I was nuts. I mean, he doesn't spray. Not that I would de-scent a skunk, but when the little guy came into the shelter and needed a home, I couldn't say no." She lifts Scrunchie to her face, making kissing noises.

Scrunchie maintains his trademark apathy.

He's probably the only male on campus who can in the face of Serena's affections.

"Right."

"But you're back now. For good." She sets Scrunchie down and straightens.

"Yeah. I'm back." I drop my bag and hug her.

We talked almost every day, but seeing her for the first time since she showed up at Jax's show two months ago, I realize how much I missed her.

"You look good," she says, pulling back and doing a little twirl thing with her fingers. I turn obediently. "Damn, waitressing was good for your ass."

"It was good for my bank account too."

"You mean I can stop taking gentleman callers to pay the milkman?" She bats her eyelashes.

"You haven't told me a thing about gentleman callers lately. Which means you have one and you like him," I point out.

Serena crosses to the kitchen and pulls out two glasses and something from our booze cabinet. "I like him. I haven't decided if I'll keep him."

"You decided to keep Scrunchie after one date."

"True. This guy's in a frat, and he's obsessed with his own face. But it is a great face, and he eats me with it. So..."

I shudder.

"Haley. I swear to God oral sex is not the apocalyptic event you think is it."

"Agree to disagree."

"Have you ever tried it?"

She sounds so aghast I need to defend my position, stat. "I can't get past the part where a guy is looking at you down there, not to mention sucking on you like a damned milkshake. Call me crazy."

Serena tosses her hair, indignant. "Whoever did that to you should be shot. That's B-minus technique at best. But you find a guy who knows how to do it..." She makes a noise low in her throat I wish I could unhear "... you'll be converted."

"I'm a pretty staunch atheist."

I take one of the cups she offers and sniff it. Definitely vodka.

It's two in the afternoon, and I'm about to point that out until she speaks again.

"What if it was Jax Jamieson?"

What the hell? It's five o'clock somewhere.

I take a long drink from the cup, wincing as I swallow. "I'm probably never going to see Jax again. If there even was the beginning of anything that would conceivably lead to milk-shake slurping, it's over."

"First, never say milkshake slurping again. EVER. Second..." The laughter that starts in her belly has me wondering if she's already had a few. "It's *so* not over."

"What are you talking about?"

"Let me spell it out for you: your dad is a huge record exec who happens to own Jax Jamieson."

I roll my eyes. "Jax is retiring."

"Artists don't cut ties with a label. The contacts your father has—"

"Cross."

"Sorry. The contacts Cross has, the money, the power? You don't turn your back on that. Even if you want to. You think you'll never see Jax Jamieson again? You're deluded."

I turn that over. I'm afraid to believe her because she might be blunt, but she's a silver-lining-girl at heart. There's every possibility I won't see Jax again except on TV or YouTube. And even then, maybe he'll recede into obscurity and stop doing media altogether.

Or maybe she's right.

Maybe he'll show up when I least expect him. Looking hot as sin with that smirk that says he knows all my secrets.

Because really, he does.

That low-grade pulsing in my gut, like a bass reverb you can't quite kick, starts up again.

Seeing him in Atlanta was totally unplanned and equally thrilling. I'm glad we weren't alone because how the hell did he get hotter?

The temptation to throw myself at him was almost impossible to resist.

"Speaking of daddy dearest," she goes on, bringing me back, "when are you going to see him?"

I carry my cup-o-relief to the couch, stepping

over Scrunchie, who likes to press himself up against the front like a fluffy pancake, and dropping onto the cushion. Serena follows me, perching on the arm at the other end. "I was going to say never. But now I'm thinking tomorrow."

As I explain what happened with my school enrolment, her eyes get progressively wider until she toes me with her sock foot.

"No way. You got kicked out of school?"

I hold up a hand. "Not kicked out! I'm facing a minor administrative hurdle."

But she's not fooled for a second. "They kicked your ass out of school. Haley Telfer—or is it Cross now?—you are a bad girl."

I groan and down the rest of my drink as she cackles.

"Why are you laughing?"

"Because you are so much cooler than even I knew. You're the daughter of a record executive, and the hottest guy in the world is strung out over you. And," she goes on before I can tell her how wrong she is, "I know you'll get out of this. And I can't wait to see how."

"I appreciate the vote of confidence. I think."

I shift off the couch and take my empty cup to the kitchen.

"Refill time?" Serena asks, hopeful.

"Nope, I gotta unpack." I grab my bag and start toward my room.

"Fine. But Wednesday, you should pick up music night," she calls after me. "I think Dale's going into withdrawal without you."

Getting a meeting with Cross the next day is easier than I expected. It's almost as if he's waiting for me.

Going to the meeting is harder than I expected.

Wicked is the way I remember, and not. I sit outside Cross's office, rereading the poster about the building and forcing myself not to tug at the hem of my T-shirt.

Nothing's changed. You're the same person you were yesterday. Four months ago. Twenty-one years ago.

"Mr. Cross will see you now."

I suck in a breath that fills my belly, as if the

ratio of oxygen to carbon dioxide in my body can save me.

Hold it as long as I can before letting it out.

I need to get back into school, or all the plans I've made will go up in smoke. I can't bartend my whole life. Not because I don't respect the work or the people I did it with, but because I want more.

Not just want. I *need* more.

This summer only increased my conviction.

I force my feet to carry me into that black-and-white room.

"I wondered how long it would take you to come." Cross's hands are folded on the desk as if he was posing for a portrait before I interrupted.

His eyes are blue and nothing like mine. His cheeks are lean.

But his chin. Maybe the nose...

"Have a seat."

I do, my gaze falling to the floor as I shift to get comfortable, landing on that giant fur rug under the conversation set. "You shoot that yourself?"

"No. Does it bother you?"

I look up at him as my fingers curl around the cold metal of the chair armrest.

"A lot of things bother me. The attention span of undergrads when you try to tell them how to reset their passwords. The state of the Middle East. When I go to the vending machine in the computer science building and my chips get stuck in that spiral thingy. What you do or don't put on your floor doesn't bother me." There's a reason I'm here, and it's not to talk about how this man is my father or how he chooses his décor. "I need a letter to the school stating I completed my term."

His brows draw together as if he's disappointed, not guilty. "You didn't complete your term."

"What are you talking about?"

"You left without notice with two remaining shows."

I glance toward the open door and back, lowering my voice. "Because I found out you were my father."

And there it is.

The statement hangs between us. I wait for him to acknowledge it, or deny it, or start talking about my mom.

Instead, he simply folds his hands on the desk in front of him. "So?"

I pick my jaw up off the floor. "So you hired me. You put me on tour. I didn't end up there because I deserved to, because I'd earned it."

"And because you resented this assumed nepotism, you left without fulfilling the terms of said agreement. And yet you expect to be compensated for it."

When he says it like that, it does sound bad.

"I made you a deal. One month counted for four. You didn't fulfill that."

"I left because of you."

"Because of me? Or because of him?"

I know he means Jax.

I shift out of the chair because suddenly the room feels too small.

My feet are soundless on the plush carpet as I turn away, finding myself face-to-face with the painting of the field. My blood pressure declines a few points.

"I want the letter, Mr. Cross."

"You have nothing to bargain with."

Two months ago, I would've turned tail and run.

Now, I'm smart enough to know that won't work.

I turn and step up to the desk, my heart hammering.

Cross wants me here. I see it in those eyes that, now that I look into them, aren't so different from mine.

"Don't I?"

His mouth curves. It's not a smile. I bet he's handsome if he ever lets the facade go. "So, you are my daughter after all."

The word has my fingers flexing. It's been so long since someone called me that, but I'm not sure I like how it sounds.

"What do you want? Sunday dinners?" My voice is smaller than I'd like.

"I want you to pay back the time you owe. A full four months."

"One semester?" Holy shit, he's insane. "I wouldn't be back in school until next semester?"

"That's right."

My hands form fists at my sides. "How is that fair? Fathers aren't supposed to blackmail their daughters."

"Life isn't fair, Haley. Case in point: you're ready to condemn me for all I've done to help you when I'm not the one you should be judging."

Cross reaches into his drawer and produces a black flash drive. The thing lies in his hand, and I stare at it as if it's a snake.

"I don't understand."

"Women will forgive Jax anything. You're no exception. But everyone does things in their darkest moments. Things that come back to haunt them." My mind races as he says, "It's yours to do with as you see fit. Consider it a gift."

Maybe Serena was right and our story isn't over.

I don't want anything this man has to offer. But I want to know more about Jax.

The idea teases me, calls to me.

I take the drive and shove it into my pocket, ignoring the glint in Cross's eye.

I turn toward the door, but a voice brings me back.

"Well? What do you say to our new deal."

"I'll think about it."

He tilts his head, and it occurs to me what he looks like. A bird.

A raven.

"I'll throw in one more gift." He spreads his hands. "Ask me. Whatever it is that's causing you to look like that, ask me."

"No." A million thoughts circle my mind like moths swarming a flame. Choosing one seems impossible. "I'm not giving you the satisfaction of asking you why you never told me who you were. Why you never came to see me. How you could you live in the same city as me my entire life and never do anything."

His dark brows pull together. "Good. Because those are the wrong questions."

I want to tell him to go fuck himself. I'm sure that's what Jax would do.

Instead, I can't help but ask, "What's the right one?"

Cross smirks.

"When you figure that out, we'll understand one another far better."

4

HALEY

"What do you think? I wrote it about working this summer and the frustration of not being able to express yourself." Dale grins expectantly as he hits pause on the track I'm listening to.

I look past him at the familiar backdrop of the café. The tables are just starting to fill for music night.

"Yeah. It must have been really intense," I say. "Working at..."

"The library," he supplies.

"Right." I try to get excited about it, but it's harder than it used to be.

I want to see things. *Do* things.

I want to take control of my destiny.

Somewhere in between helping Jerry in the sound booth and slinging beers in a country bar, I saw a glimpse of what my life could be like.

Since meeting Cross on Monday, I've decided a few things.

I'll do what he asked and finish my work for Wicked. But I'm not waiting around for him to hand me a letter.

I got my textbooks even though I'm not in class. I'll read them all so I'm ready. And I'll knock on every door of the administration until I get readmitted.

"I'm going to make you sing with us on stage one day," Dale teases, bringing me back to the cafe. "I still remember the time you rehearsed with us."

The idea of Dale making me do anything is funny, but he's so sweet I can't resist. "What the hell. I'll sit in a set."

I pack up my computer and drop my backpack backstage before going onstage. A few people clap, and I ignore the pang of dissonance. Nothing here's changed even though I have.

Being on stage reminds me of Jax, as if I'm sharing this moment with him somehow.

I didn't expect to hear from him after his tour

wrapped, but that doesn't stop me from wondering what he's doing. How he's feeling.

It's like there's a part of my body, my soul, that's gone quiet. I want to send out a signal. Make sure it's still there.

I put everything I can into the song even though I'm only half in the room.

There's a key change, and we navigate it, a little hit of dopamine in my brain as we ride the swell of it.

Then... another change.

Not in the music. In the air.

Rock stars don't chase college dropouts. It's not a story worth writing.

But my fingers tighten on the mic, and chills race down my spine, and before I open my eyes, I know.

I wonder why he's here.

I wonder what took him so long.

I wonder what he's going to do to me when I get off this stage.

Jax stands a few feet inside the door, hands in his pockets. The Astros cap is pulled low on his head, and his long-sleeved shirt hides his tattoos but not the hard lines of his body. As a result, he's drawing more than a few envious glances from around the café.

"Haley," Dale whispers, and I realize I've stopped singing.

I force myself to finish the number.

"Can we take five?" I ask the band when we're done.

I set the mic back and step off the stage before Dale can respond, my heart hammering in my ears as I cross to Jax.

Seeing him in Atlanta in his element was one thing. This time, he's in my backyard.

Somehow he owns it too, as if it's just another town, another arena.

I tilt up my chin to meet his gaze. "Do you even follow baseball, or is that just your disguise?" I ask, glancing at his hat.

"The Houston Astros are top of the AL West. Altuve is a six-time all-star. He's even shorter in person than he looks on TV."

"Right. You and Lita should go into sports broadcasting in your retirement."

"Nah. We could buy a team though."

I can't tell if he's joking. "Don't tell me you're here for the coffee, because it sucks."

"I was in town for a meeting at the label." He

shoves a hand into the pocket of his jeans, retrieves a piece of black plastic that he holds up. "You know anything about this, Hales?"

That careless, intimate way he says my name makes me shaky, but I try to stay composed. "Why would you think that?"

"There's no way Cross held onto this flash drive for the better part of the decade and decided to dangle it in front of me now."

"He gave it to me. I thought you should have it, so I had his assistant send it to you."

"About what's on it—"

"I didn't look."

His eyes widen incrementally.

"Whoa." Dale's voice makes me wince. "Anyone ever tell you you look like Jax Jamieson?"

Jax doesn't flinch. "All the time."

"Huh."

"Dale, this is my friend—"

"Leonard."

The easy deadpan has me choking back a laugh. Because, dammit, even on my home turf, I can't ignore his physical presence, or the masculine scent that makes my insides warm, or the spark in Jax's eye at our private joke.

"Dale." Dale nudges his shoulder against mine, then glances toward the stage. "We should get back to it."

Jax watches him go, hands in his pockets. "Should I be worried?"

"About that flash drive? Or about Dale?"

He pockets the flash drive, and Serena's words about Jax being hung up on me come back to me.

"Haley, you want a drink?" one of the servers interrupts, and I force myself to look at her.

"Sure. Iced tea."

"What about you?" she asks Jax, her gaze lingering on his body.

"Nah, I'm good."

"You're here for music night, you have to order something," I say. "They make good iced tea."

"Fine. Make it two." She leaves, and Jax's gaze flicks back to me.

"Jax. What are you doing here?"

He studies me a moment, like he's still trying to answer that question himself.

"We finished our last show, and I packed up to go home to Dallas, and I realized something. I like knowing where you are. What you're doing. It helps stop the voices in my head."

The iced teas show up, and we reach for them. I go for my wallet, but he shakes me off, pulling out a fifty that has her raising a brow.

"You're hearing voices, you should stalk a psych major," I say when she leaves.

Jax's gaze narrows.

I thought taking control of my life would mean no more madness, no more drama. No more obsessing over rock stars.

But here we are.

It's easy to tell myself I'm deluded, that I have a harmless crush, when the object of it isn't standing in my café looking at me with amber eyes that I swear could melt the North Pole.

Right now, it doesn't matter that he's loaded or famous or inspires rational women to regress into hormone-fueled animals bearing sparkle-glitter signs with marriage proposals.

He's just a guy who makes me feel like I'm really fucking glad to be standing here. (And equally glad I brushed my hair before coming here.)

Maybe this *is* my life. Maybe I can get back

into school and figure out how to deal with Cross and *still* enjoy the fact that for the first time...

Jax Jamieson came for me.

I smile as the huge weight melts off my chest.

"I'm glad you came tonight. *Leonard*." I lift my glass in a toast and take a long sip through the straw. "Thanks for the tea."

Before he can respond, I turn on my heel and start toward the stage.

I get three steps before his voice stops me.

"Haley."

I glance over my shoulder, raising a brow.

Jax stares at me, hands in his jeans. He looks adorably out of place as he clears his throat. "What are you doing later?"

"Yes. No. Hell no. Jesus, Hales, what is this shit?" Jax leans over me, clicking through the playlist on the computer at the campus radio station.

"Those are completely defensible song choices," I protest.

"They're crap."

Before I left for the summer, I'd promised to

cover some September shifts for a classmate going on exchange.

Now Jax's hat sits on the board, ditched now that we're inside and unlikely to be swarmed by fans. He looks completely at home in the tired task chair, leather reinforced with duct tape. His hair falls over his face in that way that makes my fingers itch to brush it aside. The long-sleeved overshirt's gone too, revealing a black T-shirt that clings to his chest and arms.

Now that we're not on tour, there aren't thousands of fans screaming for him, dozens of people catering to him, it's all so normal I can almost pretend we're just two friends hanging out.

At least until the warm light in the booth caresses his skin, the sleeve of tattoos, in a way that directly challenges my vow to keep things simple.

"You need an education," Jax goes on.

"That's why I'm at college."

"Not that kind of education. The kind I can give you."

Ignoring the way his rumbling voice sends heat down my spine, I get off my stool and hip-check him so he rolls across the floor. "What do you want me to play, O Supreme Curator of Musical Taste?"

He leans back in his chair, folding his hands behind his head so his shirt pulls across his muscled chest. "Something classic. The Smiths. AC/DC. Me."

The grin that pulls across his face is smug and sexy as hell.

Resisting Jax is nearly impossible. But the kicker is he's not offering me anything. All he's doing is being himself.

I'm trying to remember I'm here to play a mix of contemporary rock music for a bunch of undergrads who are probably watching Netflix, not launching myself at Jax like a human can of Silly String.

The whole 'he's just a guy' thing was working for me really well until this moment.

I turn back to the computer so I don't have to deal with the arousal stirring in my stomach. "No way."

His phone buzzes, and I glance back. "I sent Grace and Annie to Disney for the weekend," he says without looking up. "Then they have a suite at the Ritz in Dallas starting Monday."

"Mouse ears."

His gaze flicks to mine. "What?"

"Just watch. They'll bring you mouse ears."

He shakes his head, and I laugh.

"That's all it takes, huh? A few days off tour and the promise of some branded mouse ears."

His grin warms me through my toes. "Never said I was complicated." He shifts forward in his chair. "I gotta call Grace quick. I'll be back."

Jax steps out, and I add a new song to the queue. I watch him through the window as he talks to his sister, and I can't help but smile.

I don't know why he's here, but I'm glad.

It's like I'm on a different frequency with him. He excites me and challenges me, and sometimes scares me. But I also feel like I can be myself with him. He doesn't judge or criticize.

I add a few more songs to the list, including one I debate for agonizing seconds, because I'm afraid to wreck the vibe in here and I know on instinct that it will.

When the track changes, I swear I feel Jax's gaze through the glass.

I flush.

The sound of Jax's voice coming through the speakers has me shivering like always. But now it's like having surround sound, especially as he returns to the booth.

"'Redline,'" he says over the music.

Prickles run down my skin as he pulls the chair closer to the desk and drops into it.

He's on the radio and in front of me, and being faced with two gods is impossible.

I try to keep my voice easy. "Figured I could humor you and your big ego."

Something shifts, and it's not the song. It's his expression, the smile fading into the kind of deliberate intensity I doubt many guys in their twenties possess.

"Tell me something." His words skim along my skin, raising the hairs there. "Do you kiss him?"

It's such a jarring departure from our conversation that I have to replay his words in my mind.

"Who? Dale?"

Before I can respond, he snags the backs of my knees and pulls.

I land in his lap, my hands bracing on his chest for balance as my heartbeat explodes in my ears.

God, he's hot.

Not like that. I mean he's actually a human

furnace under the thin T-shirt. Every ridge of his abs, his chest.

"What are you doing?" It comes out like a squeak.

Jax's hands move up my thighs, slow. His touch sears me through my jeans as he strokes up my legs, my hips.

I expected him to have a reaction to playing his song.

I didn't expect *this*.

Especially when his hands sneak under my shirt to caress my lower back.

My eyes start to drift closed, and I fight it with everything I am.

Because I'm in charge of me, even when this man threatens to wipe out all my self-control.

It's not only his touch is messing with my mind—it's the look on his face. Like a starving lion sizing up the only gazelle he's seen in weeks.

"When I pulled you out of that crowd in Atlanta," Jax murmurs, "you struggled until you realized it was me."

"So?" My voice is almost normal, and I don't know how I manage it.

"So, you like it when I touch you."

How the hell did his lips get so close?

"I like it better than being groped-slash-trampled by thousands of screaming fans, yes." I swallow, reminding myself how I said I'd keep this easy. "But I'm not on your tour anymore. I can do whatever I want. Whoever I want."

Determination crosses his face as his thumbs stroke my back, making me want to arch like a cat and taking all my willpower to resist doing exactly that.

Jax's amber eyes darken, and his scent invites me closer. Every part of him in fact, from his hard legs to his chest, invites me closer.

But I'm not ready to give in. He's used to women throwing themselves at him. That's not happening here.

"I'm not your groupie, Jax."

"That's why I like you so much, Hales." The chorus sounds in the background, and he leans forward, his nose tracing the edge of my jaw in a way that has my fingers flexing on his abs, his T-shirt. "Tell me how many times you thought about it."

I let out a shaky breath. "What? My near-death experience when you almost unwrapped that Snickers in the limo?"

I'm amazed I have enough brain cells to bluff

when every part of me's living for the places our bodies touch.

"The time I unwrapped you on my bus. You fucking *melted* for me. Don't tell me you forgot."

God, his voice is intoxicating. Jax's thumb presses against my lower lip, and my mouth opens on instinct.

A slow burn starts in my breasts, travels between my thighs.

I think I'm wet before his lips claim mine.

His tongue traces my lower lip like he's outlining the shape of it. Drawing from memory.

I'd meant to pull back. To indulge in one taste, but I underestimated the strength of that first hit.

He takes advantage, and when he nips at my lip with his teeth, Jax's kiss turns hungry on a groan I want to record. Not because that sound alone would sell a million copies, but because I want there to be one copy. And I want to listen to it every night with my hand between my thighs.

I try to stay still but my fingers itch to move up his chest. They sneak over his shoulders, into his hair.

It's still harmless. Easy.

So's lying to myself, apparently.

I might be on top, but Jax is making a play for control from the second I taste him. His hands move up my back, around to my breasts.

He cups me in his hands like he wants to memorize the shape of me, and I need to slow this thing down before it spirals off into something we can't come back from.

But part of me wants to explore, to discover. To ride out these feelings, to watch them and feel them and replay them when these few precious moments of madness are over forever.

I don't know what making out feels like for normal people because I've never been normal. It's only ever been something tolerable at best to have another person's hands on me, not to mention their mouth.

This is maddening. Torture, but the kind I escape for a breath only to launch myself back into again.

The air goes dead, and it takes a good minute for the implication to sink in.

I spin around and search for a song to put on.

Then I line up the rest of the list before I shift back against the deck.

Jax watches with hooded eyes that glow like embers.

"So. Um. This is the last song of this show. Someone will be here any second to take over."

We're so far apart compared to how we were a moment ago, but it's suddenly awkward.

How could it not be?

I blurt the first thing that comes into my head.

"Serena's seeing some frat guy. She won't be home tonight; she likes the breakfast there. They always have bacon."

Stop talking about bacon.

When Jax shifts out of the chair, grabs his cap, and crosses to the other side of the booth, I know I've done something wrong.

"We need to talk."

I tuck my hair behind my ears because somehow it got wicked messy in the last five minutes. "Wow. That's ominous."

He tugs the cap down over his head.

"Let's take a walk."

———

Despite the fact it's after dark, the air's warm for September, and I tug my hair up in a bun as we step outside.

Jax glances toward me as we fall into step next to one another. "What was your mom like?"

I look up at the trees. This afternoon I'd noticed them starting to turn, the leaves tinting gold. Now they're just ghostly shadows as we cross campus. Soon, students will be pouring out of their night classes.

"Protective. But not about physical things. She was freaked out for days after I went with friends to see *Gone Girl*. She didn't know what it was about until after I got home."

"Horror movies?"

I shake my head. "It wasn't the fictional boogieman she didn't want me exposed to. More like the boundary conditions of the human mind."

"See? What do I need a psych major for when I have you?"

I can't help the smile that tugs at my lips even though I know he can't see it.

We make it the rest of the way to the edge of campus in silence. We're almost another block closer to my place by the time Jax speaks again.

"Your mom wouldn't have liked me. What's on that flash drive, Hales..." Regret tinges his voice. Tension fills his shoulders, his arms. "I did a lot of shit when I was first signed."

I hitch my backpack higher on my shoulders. "You can't scare me, Jax. I've had sex. I've smoked a joint. I've watched porn."

His soft laugh fills the darkness, as if I've made myself sound more innocent instead of less. I focus on the lines in the sidewalk.

"What I mean is it doesn't matter."

"It does because it has consequences. The kind that never end."

I can't think of anything he'd have done that would change the attraction I feel for him.

Even though that label seems too superficial for the electricity still pulsing through my veins, it's completely right. He draws me in. Pulls me toward him, on every level. Physical, emotional, intellectual. There's nothing in this world that could reverse that magnetism.

Until he utters the words that change everything.

"Annie's not my niece, Haley. She's my daughter."

I stop next to a streetlight, and Jax pulls up next to me.

We're a block from my building, but we

might as well be a mile. I reach up to yank his hat off because I need to see his face.

"What did you say?"

His hair is everywhere, and his eyes are wary and vulnerable.

I know I've misheard him. Except the look on his face tells me I haven't.

"She's my kid. Not Grace's. Annie doesn't know." The misery in his voice guts me.

"Who's her mother?"

"It doesn't matter. She tried to contact me but couldn't. She dropped Annie off with Grace. I didn't find out until months later." His words are raw, as if talking about this causes him physical pain. "Cross stopped her from contacting me. Threatened her. Eventually paid for her silence. Then he kept Grace from telling me because he told her it would ruin my future."

Facts, admissions, and observations collide in my brain, pieces clicking into place one at a time. "That's why you hate him."

"It's one reason," Jax admits. "I wanted to tell you because I like telling you things. I like that you keep my secrets. And I don't want that hanging between us."

My chest aches with disbelief, understanding, anguish.

I want to tell him this changes nothing. But that's not true. Who he is is different than who he was a moment ago.

You knew he wasn't a saint. He's not like Dale or any of the boys Serena brings to the apartment.

It's all true, but I don't know what to do with it.

A breeze sweeps the hairs on the nape of my neck, and I wrap my arms around myself.

"That's my building." I nod down the block.

Jax lets out a breath. "I should get back to the hotel."

He flips open his phone, and instincts fight inside me.

I want him to leave.

I want him to stay.

Mostly, I want to rewind to five minutes ago when I felt as though we were just two people occupying the same space and time.

"At least come in to call your car. College girls are vicious. If you got recognized out here…" I shudder. "I couldn't live with myself."

I lead the way up the walk. I'm on autopilot

as he holds the door for me, as I take the stairs first.

I let us into the apartment and take off my shoes.

He hovers in the doorway, taking up most of the frame with his body.

I'm suddenly self-conscious as I notice the neutral décor, the fake hardwood, and the white appliances.

"We've lived here since second year. It's not quite a hotel, but for students, it's practically the Four Seasons."

Jax opens his phone, then curses.

"What's wrong?"

"Grace says she emailed me a picture of them at Disney. I didn't bring my tablet to Philly."

"You can check your email in a browser if you want." I pass him my phone without hesitation, swallowing as our fingers brush.

"Thanks."

I shift a hip against the wall next to him as he types away on my phone. Waits.

Then he holds up the picture of Annie.

She and Grace are wearing wide grins and mouse ears. A third set rests in Annie's raised hands.

"Mouse ears," Jax confirms, solemn.

"Mouse ears." I can't help but smile.

I don't know how I missed it. The way he talks about her. The look on his face.

My apartment suddenly feels too small, but it's filled with warmth, not emptiness.

"Listen. You've spent the last two years living in hotels. You deserve to sleep somewhere that feels like home."

He lowers the phone, looking past me like the answer to that invitation is somewhere in the living room.

Then he tosses his hair out of his face with that easy grace that says he does it a lot, kicks off his shoes, and hangs the hat by the door.

My heart thuds dully in my chest as Jax follows me into my room.

Now that the initial shock has worn off—has it?—I'm coming to grips with the other crazy reality.

Jax Jamieson is in my apartment.

In my room.

An hour ago, his tongue was tattooing mine.

After flicking on the small light by the bed, I search in my dresser drawer for an unopened toothbrush.

"That your overnight guest drawer?"

"Huh?" I flush as I get his meaning. "Oh. I don't have a lot of overnight guests."

A brow rises under his thick fall of hair.

"I mean, I have *some* guests. Really good-looking guests." Now his mouth is twitching, and I resist the urge to face-palm.

The look on his face is starting to melt my insides, a degree at a time, until...

"I'm not sleeping with you, Jax."

Jax cocks his head, a smirk on his handsome face. The muscles in his arms leap, dragging my gaze towards his tattoos when he rubs a hand over his neck. "Because I'm a dad?"

Jesus, how is he hotter after uttering those words.

"No. Yes. I'm not sure." I wish I didn't sound like such an indecisive child right now.

But Jax just shoves his hands in his pockets, shifting back on his heels to study me.

"You're not sleeping with me tonight or ever?"

Oh God. He says it so easily. As if he's thought about both options and is soliciting my opinion.

Before I can respond, he says, "Just kidding."

I let out a whoosh of breath.

"I know it takes you a while to warm up to someone," he goes on, his voice alone making me shiver. "Which is why I'm telling you this now."

He leans in, and it's all I can do not to whine when his lips brush my ear. "I'm totally going to fuck you someday, Hales. But not until you beg me to."

Toothbrush in hand, he leaves the room.

My knees give out.

For real.

I'm sitting cross-legged on the floor of my room wondering who the hell *says* that to another person.

I hear water running in the bathroom and tug my shirt over my head.

Then manage to push myself to standing as I work off my jeans.

My body tingles as I pull on sleep shorts and a tank top.

I slide into bed, my gaze trained on the door like I'm Jason Bourne and at any second I might need to make a run for it.

By the time Jax reenters, I've got hold of myself.

He sets the flash drive on the nightstand as he meets my gaze.

I wait for him to ask if he should take the couch.

He doesn't.

Of course he doesn't, because he's Jax Jamieson.

He strips off his shirt, making my throat go dry at the sight of his muscled chest, then slides in beside me.

I could ask him to move to the living room. Or grab my pillow and leave.

Instead, I roll over and force myself to feel him next to me in the dark.

And I tell myself the lie that I can sleep.

5

I'm going to kill whoever decided to make white curtains.

Not the blackout kind with a lining. The kind the sun goes straight through, burning your retinas at ungodly hours.

I pry my eyelids open because there's no pretending I'm going back to sleep now.

The vintage Betty Boop clock over the desk says it's nine o'clock.

I've never been this awake at nine o'clock.

The room is small, and her shit is everywhere. Not in a messy way. It's more like I see glimpses of her no matter which direction I turn.

I didn't get a good look at it last night, but there's a desk, a dresser. Some art prints. A turntable in the corner with a serious vinyl collection I'm definitely checking out later.

A couple of posters, including...

Hell yes.

There I am. Next to the door.

Satisfaction works through me.

I even remember the photo shoot for that one. It'd been like pulling teeth, but now? I'm glad I did it because it means two things:

One, she's totally gotten off to me. (Which makes my day even though I've only just woken up.)

Two, I will hold this over her head for fucking *ever*.

My gaze slides over to the dresser, the folded clothes lying on top.

Hold the bus. *Is that lace?* I stretch, craning my neck to get a better look.

My toes connect with the metal bed post. "*Fuck.*"

A noise behind me makes me freeze.

I roll over, careful not to take out Haley on the way.

I'm not used to sleeping with another person. I've probably woken her already.

But Haley curls into my bare chest, asleep

and innocent as her breath heats my skin. Damn, she's pretty like this. Her dark lashes sweeping across her cheeks. Lips just parted.

I've never come clean to someone like I did last night.

I've turned it over in my head a dozen times, what is it about her that gets to me. Trying to find, in my feelings for her, my own weakness.

She's innocent, but she's not.

She's sweet, but she's not.

She's tough, but she's not, and...

How the hell did my arm get around her waist?

Because my thumb's stroking her side where her tank rode up, and Haley makes a little sound in her sleep that makes me want to fuck the mattress.

Or her. Obviously.

But that's not going to happen. I'm no prince, but I'm not shitty enough to think it's okay to show up unannounced, drop a ten-pound bomb —or technically, a seventy-pound one with red hair—then crash at a girl's place and expect sex.

Still...

My thumb brushes her skin again because I

want to hear that sound. To memorize it in case it's the only time I hear it.

Leaving the jeans on last night was a good idea.

I can take the smell of her, the warmth.

What I can't take is when her leg drapes across mine and she snuggles closer to my bare chest.

My breath is a balloon, stretching my chest. My abs flex on instinct.

My hand slides down an inch, to the top of her hip. Shit, she's soft.

Is she that soft everywhere? It seems impossible.

But it's been so long since I actually slept with someone—in a bed, their body next to mine —I can't remember.

Haley's hips rock against mine as if I have something she knows she needs.

My biceps shake from resisting, and I can't stop the groan. "You're killing me here, Hales."

I want to haul her mouth to my mouth.

I want to give her so much pleasure she can't get off without thinking of me.

I want to tell the kid at the café with the Telecaster he doesn't have a shot in hell, whether I'm here or in Australia, because she's mine.

Before I can examine that thought too closely, something fluffy brushes against my back above the covers. "What the..."

I crane my neck, twisting in the sheets.

Then I fall out of bed on my ass. "The FUCK is that doing here?!"

"What's wrong?" Haley mumbles as I scramble to standing.

"Don't move. There's a skunk."

Her eyes fly wide and she shoots straight up. "Don't kill it!"

"I'm not going to kill it. I'm going to get it out the window."

"That's Scrunchie. It's Serena's. He doesn't spray." Haley lifts him up in front of her face. The little thing blinks at her as if the light offends it.

"I'm not sure how I feel about you now." But the smile she flashes in my direction melts whatever grudge I'd begun to harbor.

She sets the skunk on the covers, and he wanders toward the foot of the bed.

"You want to shower before breakfast?" My gaze jerks back to hers. For a second, I fantasize

Haley means together, but she shifts out of bed and hands me a towel. "I'll make coffee."

She retreats toward the living room, her ass swaying under her shorts. I call after her. "Hales."

She turns back, and I grin.

"Nice poster."

I wish to God I could take a picture of the flush on her cheeks.

As I take a shower, the normalcy of the morning gets to me.

Until I find it.

Her tropical shampoo.

I mentally catalogue the brand and kind, then because my cock's complaining about the seriously short stick he drew this morning, I weigh the pros and cons of jacking off with it.

I'm only human.

Five minutes later, I'm a human pineapple.

I dry off, pull my jeans back on, along with my T-shirt, and glance at my phone. A dozen missed calls from my agent, my business manager, and Mace. Plus a notification about my charter flight back to Dallas at noon.

"Hey, Hales, can I use your phone again?" I call as I enter the kitchen.

"If you're checking email, you can do it on my computer," Haley says. "Let me grab it." She brushes past me to go back to her room. "Oh, you remember Serena, right?"

The roommate's already at the table, wearing a sweatshirt and smudged eye makeup. She finishes the waffle she's eating and crosses her arms. "I heard you stayed over last night."

"I heard you were out with some frat boy who likes bacon," I counter.

"Because I'm sure you're the poster child for good decision-making."

"You own a skunk."

She takes her plate to the sink. "Hey, Jax Jamieson?"

"Yeah, Serena... whatever your name is?"

Her expression softens. "I told her she should fuck you, okay? Don't make me look like an asshole."

She goes into what I assume is her room, shutting the door.

Before I can make sense of what just happened, Haley's back, setting the laptop on the table in front of me.

I open my email as Haley says, "You want waffles?"

"Can I get some peanuts on top?"

She sticks her tongue out at me, and I grin as I set to work on the computer.

I confirm the charter and review my meetings for this afternoon. I had a call this morning I need to reschedule also.

Grace and Annie will be getting back from Disney tomorrow. I need to make sure they're set up at the Ritz. And Annie will be starting school in another week, so I want to get her some back-to-school supplies.

I glance up to see Haley staring at me, a box of pancake mix in one hand.

No. *Ogling.*

I run a hand through my wet hair. "See something you like?"

She flushes, setting the box on the counter. She only half succeeds and has to make a grab for it as it tumbles off. Mix flies out the end and makes a powdery pile on the floor.

"I've never seen you use a computer."

"You want me to type slower?" My voice drops an octave. "I know what emojis are too. Eggplant means cock, and peach means ass."

It's ridiculous, but she brushes the dust off her hands and returns to the table. I'm thinking about shoving the computer off my lap and pulling her into it, until she's distracted by what's on the screen. "What's that?"

"My publicist sends me a digest of fan email once a week."

Her eyes light up as she grabs the computer and swings around, dropping onto the opposite chair.

Shit, this girl's hard on my ego. It's like I'm always second-most interesting to a black box.

Which only makes me like her more.

"Charlie in Wisconsin says your song saved his life." Haley's gaze moves back and forth over the screen. "Jennifer in Baltimore saw your show, and it was the best show she'd ever seen." Her mouth curves. "Obviously she never saw Leonard Cohen."

I kick her under the table, and she laughs.

A moment later, her eyes go round, and the smile disappears. "Whoa."

I straighten, shifting closer. "What's wrong?"

"This woman... she has very specific ideas of what she wants from you."

I frown. Usually the crazies don't get through the first filter.

"She really likes your mouth." Haley's face

screws up in an expression I've never seen on her.

Not possible.

But the longer I watch, the more I realize it's true.

She's jealous.

Something in me purrs. "Really?"

Haley clears her throat. "'I dream about your mouth on my body.'"

Goodbye, smugness. Hello, desire.

Heat coils low in my gut as she continues.

"'I touch myself and imagine it's you. Thinking about it makes me so wet.'"

The words roll off her lips, and every one lights new fires throughout my body.

Phrases like "touch myself" and "wet" imprint on the back of my brain, feeding the flames stroking down my spine and making my abs flex.

"'You're the hottest thing I've ever seen, and ...'"

She swallows, her brows pulling together. Her cheeks flush pink, and I should be pulling the screen back, but there's no stopping now.

I'd give every dollar I've made to hear her finish that thought.

I manage a grunted, "What?"

She doesn't disappoint.

"'When I fuck myself, I pretend it's you. Your mouth, your hands, your cock.'" Her voice catches. "'In my mind, you fuck me senseless. All night.'"

Jesus.

Every ounce of blood is now south of the 49th parallel.

Fuck waffles.

I could lower her down on this table, because God knows she's going to need something to hold onto when I strip those shorts off her hips and lose myself in her.

Haley's gaze cuts to mine, and the expression there nearly destroys me. No computer in the world can explain the way she's looking at me right now.

I know because I feel it too.

She clears her throat, but her words are still rough. "Her name is—"

"I don't want her name, Hales." My voice is a rasp. My cock might smell like pineapple, but it's saluting her like a damned oak tree under the table.

I want to see if this poor excuse for foreplay

has her as turned on as it has me. I want to force her to keep those pretty hazel eyes open so I can memorize the way they change color when I take her over the edge again and again.

Buzzzzz.

My gaze drags to my flip phone on the table, and I curse.

It's a reminder of my flight.

Maybe of my sanity.

Because what was about to go down here would've been certifiable.

I want her. More than I've wanted just about anything I can remember.

But my casual remark about fucking her last night was a slip. The product of a grueling day and the way she looked when I'd kissed her.

I never meant for things to go that far.

Grace and I used to ride our bikes down this hill as kids. It started so gradual you barely noticed, but you'd pick up speed until you were flying, careening out of control toward a blind corner.

It was the best fucking feeling on Earth.

Including the time I'd nearly been hit by a truck at the bottom.

This time, I'm not worried about hurting me. I'm worried about hurting Haley.

Problem is, I don't know how I'm going to resist her either.

If I go there with her—*if*—it'll be on my terms. When I have an iron grip on my own need and nothing to prove except that I can take her higher, deeper, better than any guy who's ever thought about touching her.

"I have to go." I shove out of my chair.

Haley rises too, her mouth forming a little O that doesn't help my self-control. "What about breakfast?"

We both look at the pile on the floor at the same time.

I try to hide the smirk.

Fail.

She laughs, and damn if that isn't what I love about being around her. Haley doesn't take herself too seriously, and when I'm with her, I can't either.

"Rain check? I need to get Annie settled and back to school. I'll be back at Wicked in a few weeks for meetings. You need anything, you know where to find me."

I cross to her, because I can't leave without

one more hit, and drop my lips to her temple. Her tiny sigh has my gut knotting again.

"See you, Hales."

"Bye, Jax."

I turn and start toward the door, stopping at the sight of the black-and-white mop between me and the foyer.

We stare each other down.

Then, as if he just realized his tail is on fire, he scurries off.

"Yeah, you better watch out."

6

HALEY

"That's it. She's dead." I sigh, looking up from the computer. "Why can't Wicked spend more on technology?"

Wendy's pale gaze runs over me. She hasn't softened much since the day I interviewed with her, but on this topic at least, we're allies.

"Most of the budget goes to the big revenue generators, like the tours. So, we have to keep what we have running."

I blow a piece of hair out of my face. We might be working overtime, but the air conditioning in the server room is definitely not on the plan.

In the week I've worked at Wicked, I've

learned a few things. Wendy runs the tech department, which is seriously understaffed at four people plus me. Though the recording tech is state-of-the-art, everything the company runs on—servers, desktop computers, the network— is old-school.

Wendy glances at the clock, which says it's almost six. "I need to go pick up my son for the weekend. Don't forget to check your employee mailbox for your paperwork."

Wendy leaves, and I wipe my brow as I look back at the stack of computers.

If Cross wanted me to do penance, I'm doing it. I got a classmate to slip me the outlines of my would-be courses for this semester. Now between working full days here, making calls and emails to try and find a loophole that will get back into school (which so far have yielded nothing), and keeping up on "my" readings and assignments? I fall into bed exhausted at night.

Which is just as well because lying awake thinking what I've been thinking isn't healthy.

Jax Jamieson groped you at the campus radio station.

Then told you he was a dad.

(Hot dad.)

You let him sleep in your bed. Use all your body wash (wtf?). Then vanish from your kitchen only to ghost you the modern way after.

Okay, the last part's not entirely true.

I texted him Saturday afternoon to make sure his plane got in.

Sunday, he emailed me a picture of Annie on a ride, wearing both sets of mouse ears, with the text "My ears get around."

But since Tuesday...

Nothing.

I try to ignore the disappointment.

"I'm totally going to fuck you someday, Hales. But not until you beg me."

It's arrogant, but after spending the summer bartending, I've had guys tell me a lot of things.

If it were any other guy, I would've kicked him out on his ass in two seconds flat—with or without Andre's help.

With Jax, I don't want to.

I want to lock the door so the world can't get in. I want to see every inch of his perfect body. I want to feel the shivers through mine.

But it's never going to happen because the thought is completely terrifying. Compared with the guys I've been physical with, Jax is like another species. Strong and hard and confident. A meteor that's going to blow me apart, leave me picking up the pieces after.

I shove off the thoughts, grab the computer I'm working on, and tuck it under my arm.

The basement's nearly empty, and it's not until I'm on the second floor that I see even a single other employee.

On the way to the mailboxes, I pass a studio and hear my name.

I stick my head in, and my grumpiness melts away as I catch sight of the last person I'd expected.

"Jerry! What are you doing here?"

My former mentor smiles up at me from his chair. Today he's wearing a long-sleeved tan shirt that makes him look like Yoda.

He basically is.

"Miss Telfer. Got a few months before the next tour. Figured I'd whip some kids into shape here."

I'm not at all sure he needs to be doing another tour, but I step into the studio and peer through the glass. My jaw drops more.

"Lita?"

"Haley!" She opens the door that separates

the artists and the producers, grinning as she leans against the doorway.

She glances down at my accessory. "Whoa. What is that?"

"Plays Betamax," Jerry offers.

"It's a computer." I swallow my grin. "You're back recording already?"

"Yeah. Were you in a sauna?"

I wipe at the sweat on my forehead. "Close. Server room."

"Huh. You should help on this album." Lita says it like it's an easy thing, but once the idea enters my brain, I can't kick it.

"That would be awesome." Being in this office and actually doing some production has adrenaline coursing through my veins. "This is the EP you were talking about this summer?"

"Yeah. I really think this could be the difference maker." Her eyes glow. "I'd love to run some of the tracks through your program."

My heart kicks in my chest. "Yeah. Sure."

She'd watched me tweak it this summer in Nashville, running version after version to optimize it the best way I could.

We catch up for a couple of minutes, then I start to the elevator.

"Shit," I mutter as the doors open, realizing I've forgotten my paperwork. I start to turn on my heel, but the man in the carriage calls out.

"Haley."

"I forgot something." I hitch my thumb over my shoulder, but Cross holds the door.

Eventually I step inside, shifting the shell of a computer under my arms so I don't drop it. "What's that?"

"A hard drive. A useless one. I was going to try to fix it this weekend."

The gray in his hair shines as he cocks his head. "You're taking company property off the premises."

"The premises will be more valuable without this."

I half expect him to send me back upstairs with the computer, but he doesn't. Cross just stands there, staring at the seam in the doors.

"I trust Wendy's keeping you busy."

"Actually, the state of this place is keeping me busy." I debate how much to say, then go all in because honesty's almost always better. "Wicked is ten years behind on hardware. Fifteen on software. You won't fall off a cliff, but it'll be a slow death if you don't start upgrading."

"Thank you for that perspective."

"I am doing everything I can," I say so it doesn't only sound like I'm complaining. "Over the next two months, we should be able to bring email and databases up to date."

He turns his gaze on me. "I was told this summer that project would take eight months and we'd have to delay other projects in order to do it."

I hesitate because I don't want to get Wendy in trouble. "Well, I think I can do it in two."

The door dings, and he strides out of the elevator.

I trot after him, which is ridiculous since two minutes ago I wouldn't get in the elevator with him. "Mr. Cross!"

"Shannon."

I look past him. There's no one around us, but clearly he doesn't want this to get out.

"What would it take for a chance to do something other than computer upgrades?"

His dark eyes say he's as intrigued as he is wary. "Such as?"

I bite my cheek. "Lita's new album. I want to work on it. I think I can make it better."

A slick Town Car approaches before gliding to a halt in front of us.

"No."

"No?" I nearly drop the hard drive but scramble and manage to catch it. "But there must be a way. I can keep doing the upgrades, do this on top. Lita already said she'd be fine with it."

"You're naive." His sharp voice cuts the humidity in the air like a knife as he stares at me over the door of his car. "I had hoped when I sent you on tour this summer that you'd prove you weren't a typical college student. That, like me, you want more and will do whatever it takes to get it. But I gave you an opportunity hundreds of students would kill for, and you ran from it. Second chances don't come easily in this world, Haley."

I lift my chin. "I don't know. I'm giving you one, aren't I?"

His expression darkens, his gaze narrowing like he smells something bad.

Then Cross slides into the car, and a moment later, it glides away.

Saturday, I'm up before noon and take Scrunchie for a walk on campus to clear my head. The grounds are quiet, but even though only a handful of students are crossing the quad, I feel apart from it.

"Haley?"

That voice has me stiffening as I turn. "Professor Carter."

His button-down and T-shirt make him look like a grad student. His blond hair is styled, his smile easy.

At least until he sees Scrunchie. "What is that?"

"Exotic cat."

"Right." He shakes his head. "I haven't heard from you in ages. Or seen you in class."

Since you refused to submit my program and hired someone else?

"There was a snag with my scheduling. I'm taking a semester off."

"Huh. Well, you look fantastic." I'm not sure he even took in my yoga pants, T-shirt, flip flops, and messy bun because his grin is automatic. Less earnest than Dale's, but it comes easier than Jax's. "I was thinking about your program. I know we missed the Spark competition, but there's a bigger one this fall that was just announced. You'd need to run more trials. Which means more data to feed the beast. But if you're serious about it, we could have it ready. The prize is twenty-five thousand. The deadline is end of October."

I glance down to where Scrunchie is tugging at his leash, eager to find the perfect grub. Carter's offer brings up a host of emotions. Flattery because he thought of me for this. Excitement because getting his eyes on this would help my chances a lot. There's likely no one else I could get with the insight to help me like he can.

But he already stepped on me once this year, and I like to think I'm not stupid.

"The exposure's even better than the money," he says. "The winner gets written up on the top tech blogs."

My gaze snaps up. "I wrote some other code this summer. An interface that helps deal with memory and attention limitations. If I win, do you think I could use the platform to raise awareness for that? Maybe find other developers to work on it?"

"I suppose." He shrugs.

"Let's do it," I decide.

"Great. Oh, while I'm at it, I got some money for a research assistant position. Do you want it?"

I ignore for a moment the fact that I'm not technically enrolled because that's something I'm going to fix soon.

Do I want to work for the most brilliant guy I've ever met? The one I've been dying to work with for the last three years?

He looks so honest, but Cross's face rises up in my mind again.

Prove to me you're smart.

Prove to me you're special.

Prove to me you want it.

I'm done proving it.

"Actually, I'm pretty busy with work. And now this competition. But thanks."

I pull up the competition info on my phone as I walk away.

By the time I get home, my mind's going a mile a minute.

Serena greets me as I enter our apartment. "Hey, roomie. Aww, you took Scrunchmuffin for a walk."

"He was scrunchmuffining my shoes. You'll never guess who I saw on campus."

"Who?"

"Carter."

Her jaw drops. "What'd he say?"

"He offered to submit my program to an even bigger competition this fall, which I'm going to do. He also asked if I wanted to be his RA. Which I'm not."

"Damn. You are a *badass* with the men. Last weekend you bring home a rock star. This weekend, you shoot down the Nerd Prince of Harvard."

"MIT."

"Whatever." She slants me a look. "I can't wait to see how you're going to top this."

"There will be no topping. I'm just tired of being pushed around. By Cross. By the university. Everyone."

"Hear, hear."

"There's one problem. I agreed to the competition before I read all the specs. I need a ton more data to test my program."

Her face screws up. "You lost me."

"Basically, I need to test how my app stacks up at creating a hit track compared to the industry's best producers. Which means I need access to a lot of tracks. With different versions, which will let me test the human's choices against my algorithm. And I don't have a lot of time. I need someone who can give me approval for a lot of hit songs at once."

"Cross?"

"That was my first thought. But no." Not without leverage anyway. "There's someone else who can."

7

"You're going to get fat."

I look up from the paperwork at the hotel lobby restaurant and nod at the empty plate in front of me. "You don't know what was on there."

"Burger. Fries. Side of pickles." Mace looms over me, his hair pulled back in a ponytail. His trademark beard has been tamed into a slick goatee.

"Tell me you're auditioning for a hipster revival of *Pirates of Penzance*."

He rubs a hand over his face. "I was going to apologize for being late. But I realized you wouldn't give a shit anyway."

"Let's go upstairs."

I shuffle the papers into the folder.

Our feet are soundless as we cross the lobby carpet. I stop at the concierge's desk on the way to the elevator. "I'm expecting someone this afternoon. Buzz them up."

"Of course, Mr. Leonard."

We ride the elevator up, and I swipe my card at my door and step inside.

Mace groans. "Nice digs."

In the final days of tour, the realtor sent me listings for three huge mansions on the outskirts of Dallas. But I didn't go to see any of them. All three felt too permanent, too big. Which led to me renting the two-bedroom penthouse of the best hotel in town.

The living room is big enough to throw a party in, with low twin couches facing one another and a dark wood table between them. Art occupies the walls. There's a TV that comes down from the ceiling at the drop of a button.

"You haven't seen the best part." I take him out to the balcony, and he whistles.

"Life is good, huh?" Mace leans over the railing.

I study the landscape, the skyline of the city. Beneath us, people bustle around.

Some days I'm not sure how Mace and I ended up playing our own songs for packed houses instead of homeless or busting our asses for minimum wage. I know what that's like because it's where I came from.

"What about your sister and Annie? Are they on this floor too?"

My mood goes to shit in two seconds. "I stopped by the house for a talk with her husband earlier this week."

His brows pull together. "You're a public figure. You'll get in a shit-ton of trouble for that."

"The asshole called Grace and said I threatened him. She left, went back to him. Annie too."

"What're you going to do?"

"I'm working on it."

That's why my lawyer's due to stop by in a couple of hours. My agent phoned around and referred me to someone local who's expensive, good, and discreet. I've spent half the week with him.

It's also why I spent this morning looking over my finances. I've got more money than I could've counted as a teenager and I'm determined not to go bankrupt like some artists. I lived enough of my life poor to know I'll never let myself end up there again.

"What do you do? Now that you're off tour."

"I see my kid. I eat food that's not from a box. I work out."

Mace grunts. "I've built the Millennium Falcon, the Y-Wing, and the snowspeeder since we got off tour. And you know what I realized?" I shake my head. "All the little yellow LEGO dudes are the same, light sabers or no." He shoves a hand through his hair.

"Maybe you need a girl."

"Fuck no. I need a *job*. I can't even remember a time before I played for a band."

I recall the dimly lit venues I'd sneak out to with friends when I could afford to. Mace was way beyond the little shows and bars—I knew it even then. That was why I asked Cross if we could bring him in when Cross made me an offer. I wanted something familiar from home.

The music, the lifestyle, seemed to be part of Mace. At the time, I hadn't realized how much.

He pulls out a pack of cigarettes, and I raise a brow. "What happened to the nicotine patches?"

"The lesser of many evils." He shoots me a

nervous smile as he lights it and takes a long drag. "When're we gonna record that album?"

Prickles of warning, twined with guilt, take up residence in my gut.

"I'm not in a hurry. Been cooped up on tour for eighteen months, man."

"Give me a date. I need something to look forward to."

I could lead him on, but I owe him better. "I don't know when. When I signed the deal with Cross to do this last album, I didn't know about Annie."

His face goes pale. "So, what? You're out for good because you want to be a family man?"

"It's not just that." I snag his cigarette and take a drag before passing it back. "The first album was me on my knees. It was never supposed to catch on. The second was me figuring out what the hell was going on in a world where I wasn't scraping for enough to buy mac and cheese. The third album—"

"It was weak," Mace says. "It was you in a power struggle with Cross. And maybe the producers saved your ass, but it was the worst thing you've put out."

I nod because he's not wrong. "I'm not

putting out another shit album for Cross, or the money, or the lawyers."

"Then make it a real album. The kind that leaves you bleeding on the floor."

He says the words as if it's never occurred to me. The possibility of doing exactly that's drifted through my mind dozens of times.

I love making music. There's no question.

But it's a toxic relationship, like mine with Cross. The songs I write that matter have all cost me something.

Some days, I wonder who I'd be if I hadn't cut those parts of me out.

My friend finishes his cigarette, and I hold the door for him to go inside.

We shoot the shit for an hour, talking about Kyle's new charity commercials and the fact that Brick bought a place down the street from Nina. We complain about music and TV and the price of beer before I finally walk him out.

I check my phone in the kitchen. The lawyer wants to reschedule because they didn't get some papers in time. Grace hasn't replied to the text I sent two days ago, and I'm edgy. I'm on strict instructions from the lawyer not to doing anything stupid—technically, I think he said don't do anything—but I haven't seen my kid all week and I'm agitated.

Another text from earlier this week catches my eye.

Haley.

Instead of responding, I turn off my phone and change into swim trunks and take the elevator down to the pool level.

The smell of chlorine when I pass through the doors hits me like a drug.

Coming off tour's like getting released from jail. You've got to have routines, or you'll destroy yourself.

Which is one reason I've swum thirty laps every day since returning to Dallas.

The place is empty, and I have my pick of lanes. I drop my towel on a chair and dive in.

There's something about water that's cleansing. It strips us all down, makes us equal.

I never paid attention to science in high school, but in these moments, I get that we're all just atoms. That when you look close enough, we're all part of the same stuff put together differently.

When I get to the end of my first lap, I hit the

wall and flip over. Front to back. Back to front. Front to back.

Somewhere between the first laps and the last, memories drift through my mind.

They start with the swimming lessons Grace and I took at the community pool as kids.

Before long, more recent ones take over.

The night Haley and I spent a night together last weekend is still the brightest thing in my mind even though all I did was hold her.

I left last week because I wasn't ready. I needed to get control of myself.

But after everything that's happened this week, that control feels more elusive than ever. Except for these moments, when I'm punishing my muscles and all I can feel is the burn deep inside them? It feels like I'm strung tight enough to snap.

I've never been selfless in bed. The blowjobs I allowed myself on tour, the way of venting when I didn't want to lose control and have another mistake, didn't help. Letting some woman I'd never see again explore her darkest fantasies with me meant I just had to be there.

I won't let myself be that with Haley. She deserves more.

She deserves everything.

We shouldn't be friends, or anything, but now that I know she exists out there in the world, I can't forget her. Maybe it would be easier if I didn't have money and fame and influence. But dammit, I'm used to getting what I want.

The thought of her seeing that Dale guy, or her precious professor, bothers the hell out of me. But at least they don't come with the baggage I have. With the distance of a few hundred miles between us, it's easier to see how true that is.

Which means that until I get my head on straight, which I can't see happening anytime soon?

The best thing I can do is stay far, far away from her.

8

HALEY

I almost chicken out three times.

The first is on the way to the airport, when I know there's no way I can score a standby flight in my price range.

Second is when I'm in the air at thirty-five thousand feet.

But the third isn't until I'm in the elevator, realizing there's no way I'll get up to the penthouse.

Outside his door, I glance at the jean skirt and tank top I put on this morning. I traded the Converse sneakers for ballet flats and flat-ironed my hair so it falls down my back. I press my lips together, but the balm I applied on my way out this morning is gone.

I knock lightly.

Nothing.

Maybe he's not home.

Disappointment seeps through me. On its heels, though, there's relief. Because not seeing him means I don't have to look him in the eye and ask him something he's not going to like.

Come on, Haley, suck it up.

This time I knock hard enough the wood hurts my knuckles.

Finally, I hear footsteps.

Then the door swings wide, spilling light into the plush but windowless hallway.

Dammit. I should've prepared myself better.

There's no guitar in his hands, no paparazzi lurking in the corner. Jax shouldn't look like a god sent to wreck havoc on mortals.

His jaw's a little shy of square, his lips carved and purposeful, as if someone created him knowing he'd use his mouth, his voice, to rock the world. His hair is damp and brushes his forehead on one side.

Jax's white undershirt shows off the muscles of his shoulders, the scrolling ink of his tattoos. He's also wearing sweatpants.

I never knew sweatpants could cause cardiac arrest before.

"Haley."

He's surprised, and it's not in a good way.

"Hi. Is there... are you with someone?" It had never occurred to me, but now, seeing the curl of his hair, uncertainty creeps in with misery on its heels.

"Mace left a while ago. I just got back from the pool." Relief has my shoulders sagging. "How'd you get up here?"

"Your doorman buzzed me up. Can I come in?"

He steps back, and I follow him inside.

I had a speech prepared, but it escapes me as I take in the foyer of his penthouse. Plush carpet, cream walls. A round mahogany table with a vase spilling fresh flowers.

It's a palace.

The thing is it doesn't seem too grand for him. It seems just right.

My attention drops to the pile of glossy magazines and brochures on the table. "Whoa, what is all this?"

"From my agent."

"A soda jingle. A reality TV series." I snort,

picturing the guy I know doing either of those. But it's the third that has my stomach shaking. "Japanese hairspray?"

"Got to keep the money flowing." His mouth twists, and I relax a degree. Despite the reality check of this environment—the room that probably costs more a night than my apartment does a month—I'm reminded that this is still Jax. The man I joked with on tour. The man whose hoodie I own.

Although he doesn't look the most relaxed at the moment. Considering he's finished his tour, back in the city he wanted so badly to return to, he looks like he's ready to go three rounds with the world.

"You said I could come if I needed something." My throat is suddenly dry. "Can I get a drink first?"

With a moment's hesitation, he turns, and I follow him to the kitchen.

I try to ignore the way his clothes hug the muscles of his back. His shoulders. His ass.

Jax reaches into the stainless fridge, pops the top on a soda water, and offers it to me.

My gaze pulls down the kitchen to the bar at the end. "Do you have anything stronger?"

He goes to the bar, returns with a bottle of bourbon. He pours two fingers into a glass, which I take.

"Thanks." Jax studies me as I tip the glass back, wincing as the bourbon burns down my throat.

Now or never.

"You remember the app I was working on this summer?" He nods. "I've got another chance to submit it to a competition. But this contest's even bigger. I need more data. Preferably early cuts. The more songs and the more variations, the better."

"Meaning?"

I take a breath. Then another drink. "I need permission to use your songs. Unedited, unreleased—"

"Absolutely not."

I played this moment out in my head. I pictured him looking incredulous. Sceptical even.

What I didn't picture was the lightning-quick response. The dismissive jerk of his head.

"It's for science, Jax. Sure, the program can help make songs that sell. More importantly, it can help us learn how music affects our brains, our feelings. I was doing some research on the plane, and there are all these networks of scientists looking to understand the links between music and our emotions. Even our development as kids. What's more worthy than that?"

"This is business, Hales. Not personal."

Fire starts in my gut, and it's not from the bourbon. "Your best friend is your bassist. You almost missed a show because your flip phone went missing and you couldn't call your daughter. You say I'm just a tech on your tour, then you say you're going to fuck me someday. So tell me again where personal ends and business begins."

Jax's gaze narrows. "This isn't a good time, Hales. I can't help you."

He brushes past me, and I set the glass on the counter, scrambling after him. When he reaches for the door, I slide between it and him.

We stare each other down.

I'm out of options.

Not quite.

Everyone wants something. Cross wants power. Carter wants... who the hell knows what Carter wants? I'm done guessing.

But Jax? I know what Jax wants.

"I'm going to fuck you someday. But not until you beg me for it."

Riding a wave of bravado I might regret, I reach for the hem of my shirt.

The irritation is gone, replaced by something like panic. "What are you doing?"

I have no idea, but they say doing the same thing and expecting different results is the definition of insanity.

Moving slowly, I drag my tank up and over my head, squirming a little when it gets stuck on my earring. "Ouch."

"You need help?"

"No." I flush red. Panting, I manage to get the shirt off.

It takes every ounce of courage in me to let the fabric fall from my fingertips.

I've never tried to seduce a man before. I've never wanted to, nor am I deluded enough to think I know the first thing about how to do it.

I don't have moves, or pornstar heels, or dirty talk.

All I have is me and the feedback from his expression, his body, to guide me. To tell me if I'm on to something or if this will ruin everything.

Testing, I inch closer.

His nostrils flare, but he can't scare me. Not when I see his gaze drop to my black satin bra and linger there.

That observation makes me bolder. It's a positive result that has me deeming this line of experiments worthy of further exploration.

"I need those songs, Jax."

I trace the line of his shoulder, biting my tongue at the feel of his hot skin beneath my finger, and his eyes darken. I can smell his shower on him, and I ignore the lust that rises up.

He's used to people tripping over themselves to obey him. He's not used to being pushed.

I'm gaining confidence in my play until everything shifts.

"You want me to pay you by the minute, Hales?" His voice is a soft challenge. Or by the act?"

I swallow, thick. "What's the norm?"

He glowers down at me like an avenging angel. "None of this is the norm. And it's not you. You don't think I know I could have you right now?"

Jax's hands grab my wrists, slam them overhead.

That's when I know I was wrong. That I took this too far.

I twist in his grip, trapped between the heat of his fingers and the door.

But instead of relenting, he squeezes harder.

I'm shaking on the inside. I hope to God he doesn't see it because I don't want to be weak in front of him. Not like this.

Jax's gaze rakes down my body. His slow perusal lingers on my lips, my breasts. My skirt's twisted and bunching, and I want to fix it.

But his gaze returns to mine, fierce and determined. "You. Need. To. Leave."

He lets go of my wrists, and they drop, limp at my sides. My head falls back, hitting the door as my eyes close.

Something soft tickles my cheek.

His hair.

I turn an inch, because that's all I can do, to find his forehead pressed against the wall.

I breathe him in, inhaling the familiar scent of his...

"Jax," I whisper.

"What?" The response is barely audible as he

turns his face toward mine, his eyelids at half-mast.

The corner of my mouth twitches. "Did you buy my shampoo?"

Those amber eyes open, slow. The look in them has me sucking in a breath too late.

Because he *devours* me.

Every woman should have a chance to be kissed by Jax Jamieson once, because I can't think of anything that compares when that sexy mouth slants over mine.

He tastes like smoke, or I do, and the flavor of Jax and bourbon is the best thing I've ever had on my tongue.

My fingers find his damp hair. Not because I'm ready for more, but because I need something to hold onto.

He presses me back into the door on a groan.

His hands grip my bare waist, stroke up my back, sending shimmering ripples of sensation across my skin.

My nipples are tight peaks rubbing against his chest through my bra, and the friction has me making stupid little sounds I wish I could swallow.

I don't know where this is going. Or maybe I

do, and that's even scarier. It's like we're racing toward a cliff and I can't decide whether to hit the brakes or the gas.

The fear in my stomach can linger, keep company with the doubt, but none of it stands a chance next to the promise in Jax's eyes.

It's not a promise of safety or security.

It's a promise to show me something I've never seen before. Something *incredible*.

Which is why suddenly I'm kissing him back, pressing into him, tangling my tongue with his.

My hands loosen their grip, running down his shoulders, exploring the muscles there.

Jax's hands run up under the hem of my skirt to the edge of my panties, grabbing my ass like it's his right. He drags my legs up around his hips, but his mouth continues to torment mine as he carries me across the living room.

Who knew Jax Jamieson was an epic multitasker?

He sets me on something soft, and I blink my eyes open.

The room, the four-poster bed, none of it can compete with the way Jax is looking down at me.

A smile ghosts across his handsome, wicked face as he tugs down the cup of my bra, his rough palm squeezing my breast. I always thought moaning during sex was something porn stars did to sell it. Now the joke's on me because I can't stop the noises coming from my throat.

"I wanted to take this slow, Hales. Make it good for you."

Before I can ask what he means, his dark head drops, and he sucks my nipple into his mouth.

Oh, God, that's crazy. I mean, it's actually *stupid* how good that feels.

He chuckles, and I think I might have said it out loud.

My hands fist in his hair, pulling him closer as he licks, bites, and sucks on my body in a way I never knew I wanted and sure as hell never would've asked for.

But he's so competent, so confident, it bleeds into me. I can't be self-conscious, can't question, because he has every answer before I can think to ask.

He pulls back, releasing my breast with a pop and moving down my body with a wicked gleam in his eye.

A sting at my hip has me pulling back as he snaps my thong against my skin. "Off."

It's a little obscene that I'm almost naked and he's still fully clothed. But then, it's like winning the lottery and complaining when they give you the cash in twenties.

I'm afraid of what's happening between us, but I'm more afraid he'll stop. That he'll shake his head and realize how crazy this is and I'll never get to touch him again.

I work the fabric down my hips, kicking it off.

He reaches for the bedside table, then drops something onto the bed. Without moving, I sneak a glance at the foil packet, and my heart rate accelerates again.

I reach for it, but he pins my hand to the covers. "No. Not yet."

I want to protest but his mouth drops to my jaw, my neck. It feels like he's everywhere. Like he has four hands instead of two, two mouths instead of one. I'm surrounded by his scent, the feel of his lips and teeth. The sounds of his shallow breathing.

This isn't what I wanted. This is torture. I'm losing myself with every touch.

His fingers trail down over my thighs to my knees.

I'm too dizzy and wanting to protest when Jax pulls my thighs apart.

This time, his gaze does drop.

Dragging down my heaving chest, my shaking stomach, settling between my legs, where he makes a noise that sounds like a growl.

Oh shit. I can take him whispering in my ear. I can take him being rough with me.

This? This I can't take.

I try to bring my legs together, but he holds them wide.

"So fucking pink," he rasps. "The things I'm going to do to you."

My stomach muscles evaporate, and I fall back onto the bed.

I'm pretty sure the difference between college guys and men can be summed up in those two sentences.

Maybe Serena's right. Maybe there's something to—

"Ohmigodstop!"

My fingers grab his hair and yank him away.

Because his *tongue* is fucking *inside* me.

"Hales?" The vibration against the most sensitive parts of me makes me squirm, but he holds me tight. "You okay?"

"Yes." My voice is tiny.

"Really?"

Jax shifts over me, and I expect confusion or even irritation.

All I find when I force my gaze to his is concern.

"No," I admit. "I don't think I'm cut out for this." I grab the top of the comforter, tugging it to cover myself.

He drops onto the bed on his side, blowing out a breath as if he's channeling patience he's never tapped before. "You know why I said I want to fuck you, Hales?"

I shake my head, slow.

"Partly, it's because I can't think of anything sexier than the feeling of you on my cock." I shiver at those words. "But mostly, it's because I want to watch you lose your mind. And I want to be the one who makes you do it. What do you think about that?"

I turn it over like it's a rational question. "I think I have no idea why you would find that satisfying," I admit. "But I like that you do."

"Good. Because if you'll let me, I will do everything in my power to make that happen."

His jaw tics, his brows drawing together in determination.

Oh boy. The idea of Jax putting his all into something—putting his all into *me*—is dizzying.

He nudges my bare shoulder with a finger. "That's what I wrote, you know," he goes on, that mouth I love curving at the corner. "On the sweatshirt. 'You're worth the wait.'"

I think I melt. "You did not write that the week after we met."

Jax grins. "How do you know?" He tucks a piece of hair behind my ear. "You want to get dressed?"

I bite my lip, considering, as my gaze runs down his still fully-clothed body. I feel like Alice stumbling into Wonderland, because the only thing I'm sure of is that if we go through with this? Nothing in my life will be normal again.

"No," I decide at last. "But maybe we could level the playing field."

He shifts off me, standing next to the bed. I prop myself up on my elbows, the blankets still draped over me.

Jax reaches for the edge of his shirt, yanking it over his head.

This is heaven. It actually is.

Heaven is this man's chest and abs and all that golden skin and rippling muscles inches from my face.

His sweatpants go next.

And whoa. That's not better at all.

I mean, it is, but it's also way more intimidating.

I stare at him. "Um. Jax... what's going on here?"

"Where exactly?" His solemn response has me shaking my head.

Because seriously.

Not only is he more of a man than any guy I've met?

He looks like one.

Every other you-know-what I've seen vanishes from my mind. Like hitting Empty Trash on your desktop.

"How is it possible we had a super awkward talk and you're still ready to go?"

He's thick and long and so hard it must ache. The bead of wetness at his tip has me swallowing.

"Because I'm always ready to where you're concerned, Hales." Jax's response is easy and shockingly earnest. "You have no idea how hard it was not to follow you to Nashville."

"Really?"

He nods, and I'm feeling less at a disadvantage every second. My gaze roams back down his body.

I shift on the bed, reaching for the foil packet at the corner as he watches. Somehow Jax's gaze darkens more when I lift it. Hold it out.

"You want me inside you?" he rasps.

"Yes."

"Say it."

"I want you inside me."

I reach for the covers over me and slowly push them to the side so I'm naked again. His gaze flares with heat as he takes me in.

"Shit, I want that too."

I watch, fascinated, as he rips into the package and rolls the condom on. He's efficient and confident, and I could watch him touch himself all day.

But that's not his plan, because he settles himself between my thighs.

"Wait! Just tell me one thing first," I say.

The concern is back, mixed with a little desperation some sick part of me loves. "Yeah?"

I blink up at him, all innocence as I tilt my head. "Do I get those tracks?"

He lets out a laugh that turns into a groan. "What'd I say about business and pleasure, Hales?"

"I don't think we came to a consensus," I murmur.

He brushes my entrance, and I swallow a moan.

I can't tell who's winning, but I love this banter. Almost as much as the sex.

"You win," he decides. "Let's talk numbers."

For a second, I wonder if I've gotten the upper hand. But the knowing look that crosses his face makes me instantly suspicious.

When he rubs a slow circle over my clit, I can't hold in the gasp.

"'Redline' as a single alone grossed fifteen mil."

The second time has pleasure shooting down my legs, making my toes clench.

"Plus a tenth of touring on the album."

My body spasms, arching up to him.

"I assume a tenth is reasonable given it was a ten-track album."

I nod, my throat working soundlessly.

He settles into a rhythm that's too slow and too intense at once.

It's good.

It's really fucking good.

And he knows *everything*. Everything he's ever made for Wicked. The hits, the flops, the sales, the tours, the press. He's like a damned encyclopedia of his career.

It's sexy.

It's maddening.

Combined with his touch, the addictive scent of him, I'm bowing off the bed, a storm building that's as familiar as it is impossible.

"You have good hands," I murmur.

His eyes glint. "I always thought they were too big."

Then he presses inside me.

"God, how many fingers is that?!"

"One." He grins, shifting to slide into me again. "Now it's two."

But I'm already gasping for breath.

"So, the unedited versions of three songs alone are worth eight figures. And that's with the friends and family discount." Jax looks up, a smirk on his handsome face as his damp hair falls across his forehead. "I assume you'll be wiring the amount in full."

All my twisted mind hears is *full*.

Because I want to be full. Of him.

I take it back. Wave the damned white flag on my naïve, careless vow to my roommate that I'm never having sex again.

I need Jax in me, or I'm going to stop breathing.

My heart will stop beating. Then I'll be dead. The first human being to die from lack of sexual satisfaction.

Serena will have to give my eulogy with Scrunchie on a leash next to her, and...

"Forget the songs," I beg.

"I thought we were making real progress."

"I'm going to rip your balls off and sell them on eBay," I mumble.

His chuckle dissolves into a grin as he shifts over me. "There's my girl," he murmurs, his lips rubbing mine and sending sparks everywhere.

I'm beyond ready for him when he presses against me, groaning.

The triumph in his eyes is overtaken by something more earnest when he nudges my legs wide.

He sinks into me.

Jax's jaw goes tight. His eyes glaze over, and it's like I'm watching a reflection of what's happening inside me.

And I get it.

Holy God, I get it now.

He's everywhere. In every part of me. My fingers, my toes, my lips, my breasts.

"Jax," I gasp. "You feel—"

"Fucking incredible," he finishes, his voice scraping along my nerve endings.

There's some discomfort, but I don't want him to go. It's like my body wants that too, and it's changing for him, around him.

Just when I think I've almost got a handle on this, he moves.

One arm bands around his body, needing to feel him, while the other fists the sheets.

I'm drifting in the sky and tethered to the ground at once.

Each thrust of his body's the verse of a song, the chapter of a story. It builds on the last, bringing us closer, sending me higher, taking him deeper.

Jax changes the angle, and my nails dig into the muscles of his neck, making him groan.

Then we're chasing each other and the feeling until I feel it build.

Or not really build, because it was there, waiting for me.

I murmur his name into his neck.

Again. And again.

My fingers dig into his shoulders because shit, it's really happening.

It's a detonation, starting in my core. Every organ's part of it, every muscle.

The waves radiate outward with an impact that registers on the Richter scale and a blast radius that probably reaches China.

I cry out something. Maybe it's his name.

I think I'm dying, and I don't really care because life doesn't get any better than this.

At least not until Jax goes tight everywhere, his back clenching beneath my fingers as he groans.

In twenty-one years, it's the most beautiful sound I've ever heard.

wo weeks. I've lived here two weeks but never noticed the pattern on the ceiling. Do all hotels have that? A big light fixture with little circles running around it?

I think I'm tripping. Every part of my body hums, from my toes to my lips. Lying on my back, my heart thudding, I catch my breath. The sheets slide under my skin as I roll onto my side.

Strands of dark hair stick to Haley's face. I can't bring myself to feel anything other than damned satisfied I made her that way. I'm pretty sure there's no way this can get better, but her eyes open and she looks at me, all dark pupils and sleepy lids.

I swear I'm immortal.

At least until Haley bursts into laughter.

I clear my throat. "Not the reaction I was going for."

But she keeps laughing. "Wow, Jax. I mean... wow."

"That I'll take." I cut off her laugh when I pull her lips to mine. I kiss her long and deep, my tongue sweeping over hers. Reminding her of what we were doing a moment ago.

What I hope we'll be doing again soon.

"You're really good at that," she murmurs when we part.

"Thanks."

I stroke her from bare shoulder all the way to her waist. I do it again—because I can—and she makes a little noise in her throat.

"I bet you've never had to talk a girl off a cliff before sex."

"I didn't have to talk you off a cliff. We just had to discuss some things."

She cocks her head, looking shy in a way that's completely adorable considering I was inside her five minutes ago. "Is that bad? Because I kind of liked the discussing part."

"It was fucking perfect." I can't help grinning. My hand skims down her chest, tugging lightly at the comforter she's holding over her chest. She drops it, watching as I cup her breast, memorizing the shape, the feel.

Obviously there are things she's more and less comfortable with, but the noise low in her throat tells me we're definitely in green-light territory.

"You're a boob guy." But her teasing has a breathy edge.

"I've always thought of myself more as an ass man. But I could be having an epiphany."

I press my lips to the underside of her breast, nipping lightly until she gasps. Then, because I can't help it, I suck her.

Hard.

"Jax..." The catch in her voice has me half-hard again already.

First things first.

I get off the bed and stride to the en suite.

As I return to the bedroom, she's like a deer caught in the headlights. All legs and eyes and innocence as she tries to slink out of bed.

"Where do you think you're going?"

"I brought some work to do."

"You came here to work?" I ask, incredulous.

"It's four in the afternoon. We're not staying in bed."

"Um, yeah, we are."

I think she's going to say no, but I manage to convince her.

Because now that she's already naked, I can take my time with her.

So I do.

I kiss her until she's breathless.

I worship her tits—which are seriously gorgeous, by the way. Not too big, but they're round and fill my hands. When I lick circles around their hardened tips, she makes the hottest fucking sounds.

Almost like when I press two fingers inside her.

This time I have more stamina.

This time, when I sink into her tight heat, I'm ready for it.

At least that's what I tell myself.

"Fuck, Hales," I groan against the soft skin of her throat.

Her arms go around me, tentative at first, then more determined. I change the angle, edging deeper, and her fingers dig into my back.

She can leave nail marks from my shoulders to my ass for all I care.

She's going to feel me for days. I don't mind her returning the favor.

I pull back to watch her face because I can't get enough of that look. Flushed cheeks, like she just got off a stage.

Full, parted lips that make me even harder.

I tell myself this girl's innocent, but the way her eyes cloud when she looks at me, when I'm inside her, I want to corrupt her.

I want to learn what she likes, then teach her every dirty thing I know and see where we end up.

When she gets close to the edge, which I can feel from the way she's breathing, how tight she is everywhere, and the little hiccups coming from her throat every few strokes, I decide I am corrupting her.

"OhhhmigodJax." The wonder in her voice makes it sound like I've just shown her a fourth dimension.

Hell, maybe I have.

That sound has my abs shaking as I run my mouth down her jaw, her throat. She arches into me.

"I fucking love seeing you like this, Hales. I love watching you come apart for me."

I know she's close, and hell, I am too, and I can't put this off anymore. So I reach down between us and rub the spot that had her leaping off the bed earlier.

Haley goes tighter than the first string on my guitar. "Oh. Oh fuck, I can't even breathe right now."

Her hoarse whisper in my ear might as well be the filthiest confession for what it does to me.

She comes around me as I continue to thrust until I can't take it anymore. I'm shaking and sweating, and the feel of her exploding around me shoves me off the edge.

I collapse on top of her and decide I want to add a new tattoo for every orgasm I give her.

"Well?" I ask when I can speak. "Was it a fluke?"

Her head swivels back and forth. "You're legit," she pants.

I can't stop the chuckle that rolls out of me.

Eventually we get dressed and go out into the living room.

We order pizza, and I pop up On Demand on the massive screen. She clicks into the recently watched list. "Home reno shows?" Her voice lifts with surprise.

"Yeah. I'd like to work on my own place someday."

"You want to build a house?"

"Maybe start with a shed. I'd be all rugged, with a saw in my hand."

"I was picturing a paint roller, maybe some wallpaper."

I'm starting to think I need to remind her of my masculinity when the pizza arrives.

She peers into the box, taking a sniff. "Whoa. What the hell is that?"

"Beef and Fritos. Best there is."

"We'll see."

But she eats it, offering a deferential nod after the first bite. "Okay, you got this one."

I grin as her attention goes back to the TV. "Well, if you're going to fix your house someday, you need one to start with."

She grabs her phone and pops up a new window with real estate listings. "How about this one?"

I glance at it. "Hales, that's pocket change. If I'm going to buy a house, it better be big."

"Right. Columns and a swimming pool." She clicks away. "How about that one?"

I start to tell her no way, but my gaze locks on the picture. "It's alright."

She hits a few keys.

"What are you doing?"

"Emailing the realtor to see if he can show it tomorrow."

"Shit. Any other parts of my life you want to fix while you're here?"

"What else needs fixing?"

I start to brush her off but think better of it.

I tell her what happened with Grace, with her husband. Haley's eyes get rounder and rounder, but she doesn't interrupt.

"I've been trying to get Grace to let me see Annie," I finish. "She said no."

"Well, it has to be a change for Grace too. You've been gone—"

"And now I'm back. And I'm going to fix things."

"Maybe she doesn't think they're broken." I turn that over in my head, uncomfortable. The light on my phone, sitting on the coffee table, blinks at us, and Haley raises a brow.

"Knock yourself out." I pass it to her, and she flips it open and scans the messages.

"How about this?" She types a message and holds it up.

When would be a good time to see Annie? I can pick her up.

I shrug. "Sure. But don't get your hopes up, Hales."

Her eyes shine. "I will do whatever I want with my hopes, Jax."

The earnestness in her expression has me shaking my head. It's cute that she's so optimistic still about the world and her place in it.

"I don't get why old guys date younger women. They can't keep up." I stiffen, realizing my mistake. "And by 'date' I mean hypothetically."

"Dammit, and here I was going to invite you to meet my father." She shoots me a look that puts me in my place.

I curse. "I deserve that. I just meant that I

didn't plan this, Hales. And you know I like being around you, but..."

"You're not looking to settle down with someone," Haley finishes. "I'm not either, Jax. I'm twenty-one. I'm just trying to live through graduation."

The words should relieve me.

When the show ends, she picks out a wildlife documentary. As I try to lose myself in it, my stomach turns over.

Not because the idea of dating her is so offensive.

Because it *isn't*.

I never thought of myself as the kind of person who'd want to date someone. I really don't even know what dating means.

My guess is it involves being in the same place as someone else for more than a few days, which for years is something I haven't been.

Plus, people who date have sex. It's pretty much guaranteed.

But they also have *this*.

The pizza and the Netflix.

The long looks and the secrets and the inside jokes.

Haley seems like the kind of woman who'd go on dates.

As opposed to the kind who shows up at your house and seduces you.

Although she was scary good at—

"Whoa!" I jerk upright so fast Haley grabs the couch for balance. "Is that a leopard?"

The thing jumps into the lake and eats an alligator.

"I told you," she says, triumphant.

"Nice ride."

"It's a Benny," Annie chirps.

I glance toward the back seat of the car I bought between my last two tours. I'm surprised Annie remembers, but it's cute.

"Actually, it's a Bentley," she corrects. "But when I was little, I couldn't *say* Bentley."

"That's fair," Haley agrees. "You like it?"

"I'd like it better in purple. Uncle Jax said they didn't come in purple."

"Maybe he'd paint it if you asked him nicely."

Her gaze meets mine in the rearview mirror, and I raise a brow.

"What's your favorite color, Haley?" my kid asks.

It's the tenth question she's asked since we picked her up, and I have no idea how she gets the energy. She's tiny and bouncy, with hair like mine and brown eyes and freckles.

"Orange."

"Uncle Jax's eyes are orange."

"Really? I hadn't noticed."

Last night, Haley and I ate pizza and binge-watched television.

Home shows. Planet Earth. Around ten, we switched to HBO.

Somehow, we fell asleep.

Not naked.

Not sweaty.

Not after I made her scream my name.

Just... asleep. I slept like the dead in a way I haven't in forever.

It was so blissfully normal I can't describe how good it felt.

I let Haley and Annie out of the car. I've been to my share of mansions. This one has a gate, a long driveway, and a dozen bedrooms.

But it's hard to focus on the specs when my attention's drawn to the way the denim shorts cling to Haley's hips and leave her long legs bare.

The T-shirt knotted at her navel teases me with the occasional glimpse of skin.

Grace had responded to Haley's text and let me take Annie for the day, which had left me both surprised and pleased.

Now I'm thinking Haley and I should've taken a detour first.

"What do you think?" I murmur.

Haley screws up her face, tapping a finger on her full lips. "No columns. Annie?"

The kid makes the same face as Haley, nodding. "No columns."

I think something's wrong with my chest. It shouldn't feel this tight hearing two girls talk about architecture.

The realtor meets us at the door.

Annie goes first, her braid bobbing down her back as she lifts her chin to look around the vaulted ceilings.

Haley looks only slightly less awed. "It didn't look this big in the listing. You could renovate one room every month and never run out."

"Of things to saw."

"Or wallpaper." Haley grins.

"It's like you've made it your job to keep my ego in check."

"Someone's got to."

The master could hold a small army. The en suite is marble with a soaker tub and a glassed-in shower. While Haley inspects the bathroom, Annie wanders off down the hall.

"What do you need a bench in the shower for?" Haley drops onto it, and I step closer. Her gaze is level with the zipper of my jeans, and she raises her chin with a startled look.

"To keep my ego in check," I repeat with a grin. I'm liking this place more and more.

I can see the wheels turn in her head. "Is that what a blowjob is really about? Ego?"

I shrug. "Depends who you ask. Some people would say it's about power. I say call it what it is: a really good fucking time."

She cocks her head. "Is it? I've never done that before."

I think I bite off my tongue.

The possibility that I could be the only man to have her gorgeous lips wrapped around me had never occurred to me. Now, it's the only thing I want in this world.

My thumb brushes her lower lip before pressing at the center. The softness of her skin, the damp heat of her mouth, has my voice dropping an octave. "I'm a good teacher."

Before she can respond, a shriek makes my blood run cold.

"Annie? Honey, where are you?"

I stalk toward the hall and pull up at a door. Haley bumps into my back. Annie's in the middle of a room that's pale purple.

"This is my room," she decides, spreading her arms as if she could touch the walls. "Haley, your room's the next one." She crooks a finger, beckoning us to follow her next door.

Haley dutifully follows her in.

"I dunno if there's enough space to put all your computer crap," I say. "But your Betty Boop clock could go right there." I nod toward one wall. "Next to your poster of me," I add with a smirk.

"Right?" Annie shoots me an exaggerated wink from the other side of the room. "Haley, what's a Betty Boob clock?"

I shake my head as Haley steps closer.

"I've been here a day, and you're asking me to move in with you?" she jokes under her breath.

"Mostly I'm angling for that blowjob."

I swear her eyes darken three shades.

"Well?" the realtor calls, breaking the spell.

"I'll take it."

Annie squeals.

"Wonderful! Let me show you the tennis courts."

I brush past him. "I don't play."

———

After we drop Annie off, I drive back to the hotel, my fingers tapping on the steering wheel.

Haley sighs out a breath, nestled in the passenger seat like she belongs there.

"You're the best dad, Jax Jamieson," she says as we pull up at a light.

The back of my throat burns. "Thanks, Hales."

"It sucks that she doesn't even know it. When are you going to tell her you're her father?"

I shoot her a look. "Grace and I agreed not to. But if I have to fight for her, I will."

"For what it's worth, I think the truth is always better. Even if it screws things up."

"You don't regret finding out about Cross."

She considers. "No. This summer, I found myself thinking I wish I'd known sooner because maybe I would've felt less alone. But then I realized being alone is good sometimes. Because no matter what happens, there are times in your life when all you have is you. And you've got to learn to have your own back."

How she got so smart I have no idea, but I'm reminded how far ahead of me she is. "You want kids someday?"

I'm really curious. More curious than I was to see the house today, though I can't put my finger on why.

"I'm not sure. I know my mom's gone and my dad was AWOL, but kids can surprise you. They can end up screwed up for no reason or amazing for no reason."

"Ain't that the truth of it."

A song comes on the radio. Lita's band.

I sing along, and Haley looks surprised. "What happened to 'Jax Jamieson doesn't do covers'?"

"I'm in the privacy of my own car. Besides," I grudgingly admit, "she's good."

"I know. I heard her recording the other day."

"What?" I slam on the brakes, and Haley sucks in a breath. "When were you going to tell me you were at Wicked?"

She shoots me a guilty look. "Cross didn't submit my letter of reference because I left the tour early. He agreed to help me get back into school on the condition I spend this semester working at Wicked."

I pull over to the side of the road, throw the car in park, and spin to face her. "No. I don't like this, Hales. You should be in school. Not in that man's debt."

"I'm keeping my options open," she corrects. "I'm going to get back into school no matter what. At least this way, if nothing else works, he'll write me the letter and I'll be back in next semester. In the meantime, I'm working. Saving up money. Submitting my program to this competition.

"He's not part of my life, and he doesn't want to be. He brought me in to assess me, and apparently he found me wanting."

Part of me wants to reach for her. Instead I drum my fingers on the steering wheel. "Hales. You should've told me."

"I was a tech on your tour. We were ships passing."

There's hurt in her voice, and I hate that I put it there.

There's a difference between control and power. Control is about directing your own life. Setting up the circumstances you interact with so things work out the way you want them to.

I've always wanted control.

I never wanted power. Power is mindless. It has no end. It exists to tempt and corrupt and enthral.

I don't want to have the power to hurt her. Because I don't want to hurt her, and because it means she can hurt me too.

Which is why I can't throw myself over the edge with her.

I need to look after myself and my kid, and for some reason I feel the need to look after Haley.

But I can't look after her if I'm falling for her.

"I need to show you something," she says before I can respond.

She shifts and pulls a scrap of paper from her pocket. I take it, scanning the handwriting.

My handwriting. "How'd you get this?"

"I found it on the floor of a diner on tour. I should've given it back, but I couldn't bring myself to. The second I read it, I knew it was a love song. And it's beautiful."

The paper's worn, like it's been folded and unfolded a million times.

I set it on the dashboard and shove a hand through my hair. "I'm never cutting another album."

"What if you change your mind?"

"I won't."

I like how much respect she has for my work. Not because she can make money off it or because she wants to suck up.

Because she just *loves* it.

"You can keep the song. And if you really want my unedited cuts for your program? They're yours." Her jaw drops. "I keep backups on a server. I can get you a drive before you leave."

Her eyes turn the color of melted chocolate. "Thank you. I'll take good care of them."

11

HALEY

Serena: You coming home at a normal time tonight?

Haley: By midnight for sure.

Serena: That's three nights in a row. Tell me you haven't given up on men and fallen in love with a computer in the basement.

Haley: Definitely not.

Serena: Good. Because the weak ass excuses you've given me since getting back aren't going to fly. I'm making popcorn tonight, and you're acting out every part of your weekend with Jax.

. . .

I got back from Dallas to an email saying half the computers at Wicked had caught a virus. I've spent every waking hour there since trying to get the systems patched and updates installed.

By Wednesday night, we're finally back up and running.

I finish up at Wicked and go home. Sure enough, Serena's parked on the couch with a notepad.

She waited up for me. And I owe her.

She slides tortoiseshell glasses onto her face as I shut the door behind me and drop my bag on the floor.

"Since when do you wear glasses?" I ask as I drop onto the couch across from her.

"Since they look super cute on me." She slides them down her nose. "First is the multiple choice. Then we'll get to the short answer and eventually the essay."

"Is this a midterm or a conversation?"

"The former. Let's get started. Did you and Jax have sex? Yes or no, please."

If I had any hope of flying under the radar,

it's gone now. I see it in her eyes. She'll bludgeon me with persistence until I cave.

Which is why I answer, "Yes."

"More than once?"

"Yes."

"*Yes*." Her eyes gleam. "Okay, equipment."

"I'm not describing his dick to you."

"How big is it?" She waits. "Blink once for small, multiple times for big."

I blink. And keep blinking.

"Now the bonus round. Did he go down on you?"

"Serena—"

"This is important." Her gaze narrows, but I refuse to look away.

"He tried," I say under my breath. "I ripped his hair out of his head when I shoved him away."

Serena chokes on a laugh. "What the hell?! Was he that bad?"

"No! It just freaked me out. It's like a guy's having a conversation with the wrong end of you."

My roommate dissolves into fits, holding her stomach. "Oh my God, Haley. And he still had sex with you after that?"

"Yeah." I sigh.

She stares at me like she's trying to read the answer from my pores. "You *came*," she accuses at last. "You came so hard."

"SERENA!"

"I told you he'd be better than Carter."

"I don't know how Carter is."

And I don't want to. All I can think about is Jax.

Not only was the sex something I'd never expected to experience in my lifetime, but house hunting with him didn't help me keep my cool.

I'd always known Jax was incredible.

I never expected him to be so *real*.

It's the realness that's killing me.

I'm not sure I can ever go back to college guys. Jax is such a... well... man. Not only his body, though God, he's in terrific shape, but the way he looks at me. The way he looks at everything. Like he knows who he is and what he can do and takes responsibility for himself in the world.

"So how did you leave things?" she asks.

"It's casual," I say, though the word feels completely wrong for describing anything that's ever happened between me and Jax. "He still has to come to Philly sometimes. And he said he'd pay for my travel if I come to visit him."

"He's paying you for booty calls!?"

I hold up a hand. "I told him no way. To the paying part, not the visiting part."

As my phone buzzes, Serena leans toward it. "Is that him?"

"No. It's..." My brows pull together. "Kyle."

"Who's Kyle? Wait, is this a fourth boyfriend?"

"No. Kyle Lithgow. The drummer for Riot Act."

"Why's he texting you?"

The answer becomes obvious.

Kyle: Lita gave me your number. I wanted to talk to you about making an album.

"What the... since when are you Dr. Dre?"

Haley: Sure. On the phone?

. . .

Kyle: I'm in Philly. Can we meet? Tomorrow?

"This is weird. I mean, Kyle's cool, but it's not like we're tight or—"

"This Kyle?" Serena holds up her phone, and I squint at the search engine image results.

"Yup. Where should I meet him?"

"The café," she says so fast my brows shoot up.

I get to the café after work at Wicked, and Serena insists on coming too. Kyle, Mace, and Lita swing in the door at the same time.

I introduce them, and we get back to the subject at hand.

"We want to do another album," Kyle says, his gaze lingering a little too long on Serena. "Jax is out, but we're still in."

Lita leans forward. "You know Cross."

I frown. "He won't even let me work on your album."

Kyle shifts in his seat. "I know you guys have a… relationship. Maybe you could talk to him."

"I didn't know that was public knowledge"—I shoot Lita a look, and she winces—"but still... you guys would make a great album. I know it. But I have zero pull."

"Doesn't hurt to try, does it?"

Their pleading faces make me sigh. "The thing is marketing's downsizing and everyone's way behind. Plus, there's no money in albums, right? It's all in touring."

"The money doesn't fucking matter." Mace's explosion has us all turning toward him.

"What my colleague means to say"—Kyle claps his friend on the shoulder with a warning look—"is that our needs are more modest than Jax's. If Jax wants to stop being a rock star, that's his deal. We need a way to keep doing it."

I turn it over in my head, but it's Serena who leans in. "You could release singles. Build a story, like an album but one piece at a time."

"Thanks, Jay-Z," I say, and she rolls her eyes. "But Cross won't go for it. If I talk to him, he'll be less likely to say yes, not more."

Mace shoves out of his chair before I can take another breath.

"Just try, okay?" Kyle asks, a pleading look on

his face before he trails his bandmate out the
door.

"Hi, Hales."

There's nothing better than answering the phone when Jax Jamieson is on the other end.

Oh, wait. There is, and it's answering a video call to find not only his gorgeous face and smirk on the other end, but damp hair curling at his ears and a tantalizing glimpse of bare shoulders and pecs.

"Why are you shirtless?"

"Just practicing for an underwear campaign."

Two emotions slam into me in quick succession. The first is lust. The second might be jealousy.

"Seriously?"

"Nah. Just got back from a swim and got out of the shower."

Now I'm picturing his hard body cutting through the water. That's way less distracting.

"What're you doing?"

"Ducked out of Wicked to work on my program." I shift on my bed, shoving my hair out of my face. "Carter gave me some feedback. Now I'm even running some of Lita's songs through the program to make suggestions. Thanks again for your data."

"Ouch. I have fifteen Billboard top tens, and all I am to you is data?"

"Not only data. But also data," I say helpfully.

His amber gaze narrows. "I think what you really want is me telling you I spent the whole call with my agent yesterday staring at the balcony and picturing what it'd be like to fuck you on it."

I nearly drop the phone.

I close the bedroom door before shifting back on my bed, pulling my knees up to my chest. Serena's outside, and if she heard that, I'm never going to see the end of it.

"That's very specific," I say.

His mouth twitches, like maybe he knows it

took me every ounce of courage to respond. "I bet you're wet just thinking about it."

Jax's smooth voice gets rough, and if I wasn't before, I am now.

Sex with Jax last weekend made me realize how much I have to learn. That part wasn't a surprise.

The surprising part was how much I *want* to.

I was afraid I might regret it. I don't. But I'm thinking about this whole other world that experienced rock stars know that I've never considered. A world where you can say as much with your bodies as with your words.

"Show me," he says.

"What?"

"Show me how wet you are."

I suck in a breath.

It's as if Jax is constantly feeling out my comfort zone. He walks around it, taking it all in, like he walks around a stage before a show until he knows every corner, every boundary.

Then he shoves me out of it.

This request is less scary than some of the things we've done because I'm totally in control and he's not even here.

On the other hand... it's completely filthy.

I stretch my legs out an inch at a time, my feet sticking on the comforter. Then I slide my hands down the front of my pants, brush the slick skin between my legs, and hold up my glistening fingertips.

"Good girl." His raspy voice isn't enough reward. Not nearly. "Now spread your legs."

Something occurs to me. "Jax, is this actually why you called? Or are you just annoyed I was talking to Carter?"

Jax's grin turns wolfish. "Both. Now touch yourself. Nice and easy."

His smugness transforms into need as I shift on the bed, adjusting the phone so I can drop my other hand back down my body.

He shifts too, and the headboard appears behind him.

Now I'm wondering if he's hard.

I'm wondering if he's leaking.

I wonder when I became the kind of girl who wondered about those things.

"What about you?" I murmur as my fingers drift over my skin.

"What about me?"

But his jaw clenches and he angles the phone down. I can see his hand on his cock, protruding from the fly of his jeans. He's thick and pink and my throat dries instantly.

He strokes himself a couple of times, his big hand firm on his cock, and that makes me wetter.

It's the dirtiest dream I've ever had. Except it's real.

"Fuck yourself. Two fingers," he commands when the camera returns to his tight face.

I do as he says, my back arching as I picture his hand, not mine.

"If you were here, I'd play with that perfect pussy."

I press against my fingers, gasping as I picture exactly that.

"One day, Hales, I'm going to take that little clit in my mouth." My thumb is a slave to his words, finding that spot, rubbing a circle, and my hips jerk against the pressure. "I'm going to suck on it until you're begging to come."

And that puts me over the edge.

I whimper as my climax shakes through me. His grunts come over the phone, and the tension in his face tells me he's almost there too. The sound of his hand sliding up and down his cock faster, harder, is hot as hell. A moment later, with a guttural groan, he comes.

I watch, fascinated. And the satisfaction from watching his face is different from my own orgasm, but it's not less. In some ways, it's more.

"Don't move." He shifts in the picture, his lids lowering like he's cleaning up. "I've been picturing that all week," he says when he finishes.

The shiver that works through me is involuntary. I don't know why that's so hot that I made him messy, but it is.

Jax props a hand behind his head, revealing a deliciously tattooed arm as he grins. "I'm in town next week. Some paperwork to finish up with Wicked."

I swear my hand shoots up in the air like I'm in second grade.

"You could stay here."

Jax hesitates, and for a second, I think he's going to say no. Instead, he says, "Perfect."

Warmth tingles in my chest. Not in a sex way.

In a feelings way.

I know him staying here doesn't mean anything. I love spending time with him even though it still feels *Sixth Sense* weird that one of the biggest stars on the planet spends his private moments with me.

Add to that the *way* we spend those moments?

It's pretty freaking great.

Especially when that guy also writes incredible songs, looks out for his friends and family, and uses the most beautiful voice to say the dirtiest things.

"I better go get ready," I say finally even though I don't want to.

"Where are you going tonight?"

"Out."

"Yes, I figured. With?"

I don't want to be evasive, but I know he won't like the answer. "Cross."

Storm clouds take over his expression as I tell him about Kyle and Mace wanting to record an album.

"They never should've come to you."

"Well, they did." I shift off the bed and prop the phone on my dresser as I rummage for new clothes. I strip out of my jeans and grab a skirt.

"It's a bad idea," he says, peering downward as if he can see below the frame of the phone.

I hide my smile. "Your opinion is noted. Goodnight, Jax."

Jax sighs, his gaze returning to mine. "You're really trying to piss me off, aren't you?"

"I let you watch me masturbate. I'd call that exceedingly accommodating."

An hour later, I make my way across town to the historic district of the city as the sun sets in the background.

The only way to make an evening out with your recently discovered record exec and control freak father more awkward is knowing you just had phone sex with your non-boyfriend.

Who works for your dad and hates him.

It's just like real family.

I sit on the edge of a concrete flower bed in front of our designated meeting spot and check my phone.

"Haley."

It takes a second for me to focus on the man in a navy button-down and jeans in front of me.

"I didn't notice you with the..." I gesture at his outfit.

"I do get out of a suit every now and then."

"Right."

"I was surprised when you suggested we talk. Away from the studio."

"Well, I was surprised you suggested here." I shift off the flowerbed and glance down the street. "Jazz?"

"This concert series has been happening for years. I had a hand in it once."

I'm not sure what to read into that. But it makes me think of how there're no pictures of him or his achievements in his office. He sticks his hands in his pockets as we walk side by side through the crowd of early-evening pedestrians.

Now that I have him here, I'm not sure what to say. I can't exactly lead with Kyle and Mace's request. Cross is way too smart for that.

"Is this what you do when you're not working?" I ask instead. "I mean, I know nothing about you."

"That's not true," he chastises.

"All right, I found out you have a brother in California." I pause. "Do you have a girlfriend?"

"No."

I go to shove my hands in my pockets, realizing my skirt has none. "What made you get into music?"

"I thought I'd play trumpet in a jazz band."

My gaze cuts to him without warning. "No way."

"Mhmm. It was all very romantic." His mouth twitches, and for a moment he looks younger.

I have to remind myself I didn't come to hear him talk about growing up. That this entire meeting is means to an end, a reason to make Kyle and Mace's request.

"So what made you decide not to play trumpet?"

"I was ten when we moved to Philadelphia from Belfast. My father had a leather goods store back in Ireland. He was a sought-after craftsman there, but when he left, he had nothing. Stateside, he worked repairing shoes. But he made sure we had enough. I always remembered what he gave up for us. I wanted to make something from his legacy."

"Which is why you started Wicked?"

He nods. "I understand what it's like to want something bigger than yourself."

It's as if he knows what's in my head. It's disconcerting as hell, but somehow it's also comforting.

I can't help asking, "What about my mom?"

Cross's mouth pulls down at the corner, but

not in a frown. More like he's trying to decide how to talk about something he's not used to talking about. "We had a relationship—an affair —for a few months. I could tell you it was serious. That I loved her. But that would be doing you a disservice. What I can say is you have her hair, her mouth, and her way of figuring things out no matter what comes your way."

I swallow because I didn't expect such a real answer from him. "When did you find out about me?"

"She told me she was pregnant. That I had to decide whether I wanted to be a father or not. There was no middle ground. My focus was my company. But I said I would support you."

This is news to me. "And did you?"

He shakes his head. "She wouldn't allow it."

This is so not why I'm here, but now that we're rolling, I can't seem to stop. I'd always pictured Shannon Cross as this untouchable executive. Not a refreshingly honest man with a lifetime love of the trumpet.

A man I'm suddenly dying to know more about.

"So you never tried to see me?"

"I did. We reconnected when you were a

teenager. Spent time together for a few weeks." *The picture from the party Serena found.* "I'd started Wicked, was working around the clock trying to discover big talent.

"I asked if I could see you. She wasn't sure at first but eventually agreed. I was in the car to go see you when I got a call. From a jail. In Dallas."

Understanding dawns. "Jax."

He nods. "I'd been trying to sign him all year. Since his eighteenth birthday. But that was the day he hit rock bottom. He had no one to help him get out of there. So I went to him instead of you."

My chest tightens. "Because you wanted to sign him."

Cross rubs a hand over his smooth jaw, a move that's startlingly familiar. "He was lost, Haley. Gutted. A child with nothing but feelings, and those feelings were eating him alive.

"Some people are live wires, meant to electrify the night." He nods at the lights hanging from the trees. "But they need careful management so they don't burn out, or catch fire, or destroy themselves."

"Jax doesn't need that anymore."

"You may be right," he surprises me by saying.

"I know Jax is supposed to do another album. What if he doesn't want to? I mean, could he get out of it?"

"Legally, it's next to impossible."

"What would he have to do?"

Dark eyes meet mine, and there's so much more in them than I ever gave him credit for. Pride and intelligence, yes. But other things I can't name. Things I hope someone will see in my eyes someday.

"He'd have to ask," Cross says finally.

When he pulls up, I realize we've entered a square with café sets. Chairs and tables, half of them occupied.

A band is setting up at one end. I can spot a clarinet, a saxophone, a double bass, and a trumpet.

Cross pulls out an empty chair, and I slide into it.

I watch him round the table, gracefully taking his seat on the other side.

The saxophonist starts warming up, and Cross's gaze locks onto the stage. It's as if the beauty of the square falls away. There are no more stones, no more flowers, no more trees, no more lights. In his mind, it's just the notes.

"You care, don't you?" I say. "About Jax."

"Of course I care. All my artists matter."

"But Jax matters more."

Cross doesn't turn, but I know he hears me.

He doesn't answer for a long time. When he does, he's drifted.

"It's ironic, in a way, that Jax is the person who kept you from me. And now he's the one who's brought you back."

The double bass starts its mellow notes that warm my stomach, and soon the trumpet joins in.

I turn his words over in my mind as the band plays.

13

"Wow. Where is everyone?"

"It's just us, squirt. Grace said you went swimming at school last week, and I thought you might want to do some more. Now go change into your swimsuit. I'll meet you back here."

The local wave pool feels cavernous. Not just because of the high ceilings, but because I rented it out.

The idea came to me when Haley said she was spending the evening with Cross. She's seen as much of her estranged father as I've seen of my kid lately.

That ends now.

As we get into the water, Annie looks nervous.

"Something wrong?" I ask.

"When we went for school, I didn't swim. I sat in the corner."

That catches me off guard. "Grace said you love water. You take baths all the time."

"That's different."

I turn it over in my head. "Come on."

We get out of the pool, and I gesture up to the operator who's watching from above. I slice across my neck. Then I leave Annie by the pool and go out to the main desk in the deserted lobby.

The lone person there is doing paperwork. "Yes, Mr. Leonard?"

"I'm going to need some of those things." I point at my bicep.

"I'm sorry?"

"You know." I flap my arms, irritated.

"Ah. Water wings?"

"Yeah, those."

She goes into the office and comes back. "Here's a set."

"I need one more."

She complies and returns, smiling. "It's very sweet that you did this for your daughter."

I start to say, "She's my niece," but catch myself. Calling her my daughter is the truth. And the more I turn it over in my head, the more I want it to be the truth. The more I want everyone to know it.

Including Annie.

I go back to the pool and hand a set of water wings to Annie.

She shakes her head. "I don't need those. I'm too old."

"Sure. But I need them."

I start blowing them up as she watches. "Really?"

"Yeah. I can't believe I almost forgot them."

It takes two seconds to realize there's no way they'll fit over my biceps. So I deflate them most of the way and wedge my hands inside so they're ugly orange bracelets.

"Fine, I guess I'll wear them too."

I hide the smile as we blow hers up.

We go back out into the water, and I show her how to paddle. The pool's still and empty, and it's just us in the shallow end.

"What is all that?" she asks, nodding to my arm.

I glance down at the ink. "Tattoos."

"I know that. What do they mean?"

"Who says tattoos need to mean something?"

"Why else would you paint something on your body you can't take off? My friend Jamie's mom let her dye her hair with permanent dye. But even that didn't last forever. This is like… forever forever." Her head bobs with her words, her eyes going round.

"It is forever forever," I agree. "Alright, the first one I got was here." I point to the knot on my shoulder. "I got it when I first became a musician because I felt like I was part of something." My finger moves to a heart under my tricep. "This one is for your mom. Because she's always been part of me, even when I don't see her." I move down my arm, scrolling past half a dozen and stopping on an elephant. "This one—"

"An elephant!" she exclaims. "Because an elephant never forgets and you never forget a song?"

"Sure," I say. "And because my friend Mace dared me to. By the time you have a lot of tattoos, the bar just gets lower."

"What bar?"

After another ten minutes of this, I can tell she's relaxed.

We've been in here a while, but her teeth aren't chattering, and she doesn't look worried, so I think we're good.

"My turn to ask questions. You still reading *Harry Potter*?" I ask.

"Yeah. I'm on book five."

"Which one's your favorite?"

"*Goblet of Fire*," she parrots immediately.

"Why?"

Annie blinks at me like I'm being deliberately slow. "Because... dragons."

"Right." I swallow the laugh. "The Fireball's the best."

"No way. The Horntail."

"You're just saying that because it's Harry's."

"Am not!"

I never pictured myself debating *Harry Potter* with a ten-year-old.

Or reading the books so that I could.

"You know how in *Harry Potter*," I say eventually, "there're a lot of changes and surprises?"

"Like Harry finding out he's a wizard?"

"Yeah, like that." I swallow. "Though this is more like *Star Wars*..."

"I haven't read that."

"Me either." *Fuck, could this be any more awkward?*

She looks so attentive, so hopeful.

I want to tell her. To spill everything that's building up inside me, all of the emotion and the frustration that I thought would go away once I was back here.

It's not going away.

Instead, I help her out of the pool, discarding our water wings.

"Go get dressed. I'll take you home. Maybe we can get ice cream on the way."

If her happy chatter between bites of our frozen Snickers treats is any indication, she's had a good time.

When we pull up at her house, Grace's sitting in one of the two chairs on the porch that looks as if it was built a century ago and hasn't been attended to since. As a kid, I wouldn't have noticed such things. But after living in hotels, I can't help it.

"Where's the man of the house?" I ask.

She lifts a shoulder. "Out with friends."

"Shocking."

Grace shoots me a warning look. "Annie, time to get ready for bed, honey."

"I'm not tired. We just had ice cream."

I put on my most innocent expression. But I'm her older brother and I never was much for innocent to begin with.

Grace rolls her eyes at me. "Put your bathing suit on the washing machine and get ready for bed. I'll come say good night in a few minutes."

I hug Annie good night, then after she goes inside, I drop into the chair opposite Grace. "I almost told her." I pick at the peeling plastic on the arm of the chair.

Grace stiffens. "You have no right."

It's an old argument, but we haven't had it face-to-face in a while.

We're due.

"No? My child is being raised by a man who doesn't respect women."

She flinches. "She's not only your child. She never was."

"And that's my fault? You kept it from me."

"I took care of things. Like you took care of me."

I didn't take care of you, I want to say. *You're here, aren't you?*

She sips tea as if we're talking about movies instead of her abusive husband. "I know this isn't the life you want for her, but life doesn't always turn out how you plan."

"I want to fix that. That's all I'm trying to do."

She lifts her chin, and for a minute, I see her when she was younger, mouthing off to me. "You have any plans to get your own life, brother?"

"What are you talking about?"

"I'm talking about the fact that for ten years, you had the biggest life imaginable. And now, everything you want is about that little girl. She can't hold the burden of your dreams, Jax. It's too much for her."

I shift, remembering what I'd said to Mace about him needing to find something new.

"I understand that you want to take this slow," I say after a moment of easy silence. "But I want her in my life. I want to provide for her in every way I can. Nothing will keep me from that. Not your husband. Not the law. Not the last ten years. Annie's my daughter, and there's no changing it."

A noise inside makes us both turn.

"What are you talking about?" a small voice says from behind the screen door.

Shit.

"Annie, honey." Grace's voice is calm, but there's an edge beneath the surface. "What are you doing out here?"

"You were taking too long." Her gaze moves between Grace and me, but my heart is racing. "Uncle Jax, what's going on?"

"How much did you hear?" My voice sounds tight.

"You said that I'm your daughter. But that's not right."

Shit. Shit. Shit.

Grace kneels in front of Annie. "Honey, this isn't how I wanted to tell you."

"How is that possible?"

"In one sense, yes, Jax is your father. In another sense, your daddy and I are your parents. And all you need to know is that you are loved."

"But who was my daddy first?"

"I was," I say before Grace can interject.

Annie's face changes as she looks at me. "Then why did you give me a new daddy?"

Pain slices though me. I don't know what to

say. All I can say is, "I'm sorry. Annie, I'm so sorry."

Her gaze flicks between us, then to the street. "I'm going to bed."

"Okay. You want to read something together?"

"No." Her voice is unusually sharp. "No. I'm going to read to myself."

Annie retreats, the screen door clicking behind her, and I rub both hands over my face.

It doesn't help. Because when I blink my eyes open, I've still fucked everything up.

14

HALEY

T

he line at the registrar's office shouldn't be this long. It's the middle of the semester. Everyone's already registered, right?

I shift because my foot's fallen asleep again. I'd rather be at Wicked right now, where I know Lita's recording. But no. I'm getting back into school, and I'm not taking no for an answer.

The number called is 473. I'm 474.

Then, it's my turn.

I get to the window. "Hi, I'm Haley Telfer. I spoke to someone about getting back into school. Here's the reference letter." I hand the woman the sealed envelope.

I haven't seen Cross since our father-daughter date earlier this week, but I found this in my mailbox with a note.

In some ways, it feels like the best gift I've ever gotten.

She opens it and scans the letter. "It says the reference is for Haley Cross."

I wince. "My name is Haley Telfer. But this is my reference."

"From a Shannon Cross. Are you related?"

"Technically he's my father. Why?"

She sets the letter on the desk. "You can't have a reference letter from a family member."

"I didn't know that man was my father until a few months ago. Not while I worked for him."

She stares at me as if I'm crazy. "Miss Telfer—Cross—whatever your name is, you are ineligible to return to this institution until you have appropriate paperwork. From a non-family member."

"You have no idea what I did to get this," I whisper.

She looks past me. "There are other people in line."

"Do you have a daughter? Does she have dreams?" I try, desperate.

"I do. And she does. Neither of which are relevant to this conversation. Next!"

As I take my letter back and trudge out of the office, the full weight of disappointment hits me.

It's a month into the fall semester, and I'm no closer to getting re-enrolled.

Which maybe is for the best since I'm behind on my readings thanks to the IT breakdowns at Wicked recently.

I need to talk to someone. I can't call Serena because she's in class. Outside, I dial Jax's number.

He answers on the third ring. "Yeah?"

I swallow, sinking onto a bench. "Jax? I didn't get back into school. Cross gave me the letter, and I still couldn't get back in." I curse. "Maybe I should just drop out."

"Maybe you should." I blink at the spot where the grass meets the cobblestone. "Hales?"

"No. It's just... I figured you'd give me a pep talk or something."

"Why?"

I'm not sure.

Jax isn't my boyfriend.

It's not his job to be there, even though he is. To comfort me, even though he does.

"Hales," he goes on, sighing out a breath, "I'm good at talking about shit that's fucked up. I'm not good at fixing it. If anything, I'm better at breaking it."

Alarm bells light up in my mind. "What happened?"

"Annie found out I'm her father. And not how I planned to tell her. Now Grace's pissed, but it's Annie who won't speak to me."

"She'll get past it."

"Did you?"

I shift. "Maybe I will."

My phone beeps, and I glance at the call waiting. "It's Lita."

Kyle's been texting all week to get an update on how my conversation with Cross went about the album.

Guilt edges in because I hadn't even gone there.

This is probably Lita's attempt. I can't avoid it forever.

"Jax, I should go. Can we talk later?"

"Yeah. Sure." But he's distant, and I don't know how to change that.

Maybe there's no way to help it.

Because he's in Dallas and I'm here, and

maybe all we can ever be at a distance is people who get each other off.

On that depressing note...

I switch lines, trying to shove it from my mind. "Hi, Lita. Sorry I didn't return your calls, but—"

She makes a strangled sound. "Haley."

"What's wrong? Where are you?"

"Something happened."

Hospitals are all the same. Linoleum and bright lights. Black streaks marking the floors, like people were drag racing with gurneys.

I'm pretty sure that never happens except on TV.

Next to me, Kyle's staring at the wall. Lita paces. Brick's wandering the halls.

It's been seven hours since I arrived.

I'm not good with hospitals. Especially this hospital.

I bury myself in my phone, trying to read articles and pretending I can focus on something other than the background noises of beeping, the staccato voices, and the occasional metal on metal.

In some ways, it shouldn't be that different from being on tour.

It's completely different from being on tour.

I glance at the clock. It's the same kind as in schools. The institutional one with a big face, blunt hands that always move too slow.

Movement catches my eye as Jax rounds the corner.

We all straighten. "Well?" I ask.

The man in a white lab coat with a buzzed head appears behind him, addressing all of us. "Your friend is going to survive."

"Mace stepped off the roof of the studio," Kyle says it loudly, and I wince. "That's not something you bounce back from."

The doctor says, "He has a broken leg, wrist, and collarbone. It could have been more severe. My suggestion is that you all get a good night's sleep and return in the morning."

I stand, weary. "Wanna go?"

Jax nods, and the four of us leave the hospital together.

A few minutes later, the black Town Car rolls up.

We drop Lita off first. Then Kyle off at his hotel.

Jax stares at the seat the rest of the way back to my place. When we get inside, Serena's reading a book.

The old-fashioned kind with a spine and everything.

Her worried face peers up at us from the couch.

"Jax. When did you get here?"

"About two hours ago. Chartered a plane." His voice sounds as if he's been up all week.

"How is he? What hospital is he at?" she asks.

I tell her, and she sets the book on the table in front of her with a sigh.

"Haley..."

"It's fine," I say, shaking my head. "Thanks, Serena."

I start toward my room. Halfway there, I realize Jax isn't following me. He's still standing by the door. I take his hand and tug him along.

I shut my door after us. Jax walks around the room, studying my things.

"I don't know what makes someone decide to..." My voice echoes in the silence, and I take a breath.

He stands in front of me, his hair falling in his face. "This isn't the first time."

"What?"

His amber eyes are dull. "It's been years. I didn't know he was in this place again."

Jax and I have talked about our pasts, but this is different. I sense it from the way his shoulders slump. The defeat in his expression.

"What happened last time?"

"Touring got to him. He was partying too much. Always chasing the latest high. We were supposed to meet up on an off day. I found him lying in the gutter in NOLA. Got him to a hospital, found needle tracks up his arms. I didn't know. I mean, on some level I knew, but I didn't know it was that bad."

"Did he mean to...?"

"I don't know. Guess this time he decided he did."

My eyes sting, and I wipe at them. "He and Kyle came to me about doing an album. I told them I'd help. That I'd talk to Cross. But I didn't, Jax. I should've, and I didn't."

"It's not your fault, Hales," he murmurs. "What did Serena mean about the hospital?"

I take a shuddering breath. "It's where my mom died."

Jax closes the distance between us.

I've hugged him before, but this time, he's the one folding me into his arms. I feel myself crumble, and I'm pissed at myself because I should be the one there for him.

"Let's take a shower," he says against my hair. I nod, slow.

Jax pulls back a few inches. Just enough to strip his T-shirt over his head. Then tugs off his jeans, his shorts.

I follow suit.

When we finally step under the spray together, I can't help noticing his body despite everything that's happened.

My gaze rakes down his back, his ass, his legs as the water runs over him. Darkening his hair to chocolate. He turns to face me, and the pull is there.

I squirt body wash into my palm and wash the hard muscles of his chest. His intake of breath is the only sign he's resisting, but he doesn't stop me.

I move around to wash his back. Every part of him is beautiful. The dark hair, soaked and curling at his neck. The breadth of his shoulders, the taper of his waist. The slim hips, the firm curve of his ass.

I turn back to the front of him, and his gaze is darker.

"Here." He takes the body wash and soaps up my shoulders, my chest, my breasts.

Jax's big hands glide down my sides, my butt. He pulls me closer, and he's half-hard. I tip my face up to his, and his mouth finds mine.

We kiss out of shared sadness. Out of desperation. Out of need to make something that's not awful.

I pull back, catching my breath. "I should've done something more. I could've helped, could've convinced Cross. I had no idea..."

"Don't blame yourself, Hales. You can get caught up in it. And once you do, you never let it go." When he speaks again, his voice is a murmur over the sound of water hitting tile. "You taught me something—there's always a choice. No matter how bad things look, you get to decide. Maybe you can't decide for the world, but you can decide how you act. How you feel."

Jax has shown his anger, his self-loathing. Never his sadness.

My hands cup the sides of his face, water running over our skin. "Promise me something. Don't ever regret me. Don't ever feel guilty. Don't wish away a moment of this. No matter what happens." He doesn't respond, and I kiss him once, hard. "*Promise*."

Jax nods, slow.

When he backs me into the tile, my heart's hammering because I want him so badly I ache with it.

Everywhere he touches me glows. The press of his cock against my stomach has me moaning against him.

His mouth crushes mine, and this time, there's no question of his intent.

For tonight, there are no walls. Neither of us can manage to keep them up.

He's going to take everything I have and am.

And I'm going to give it to him.

His expression flares with heat and something else. Jax lifts me, pressing me against the tile and leaving my legs useless. I hook them around him. When he sinks inside me, we gasp together.

His length fills me.

His soul fills me.

He strokes into me, and I want this, I need it, but it's too much. Tears burn the backs of my eyes, and I squeeze them shut.

Neither of us is ready to last long. He pumps into me, long, slow strokes, but the groans torn from his throat tell me he's close. I am too.

"Can't take it," he utters.

"I know." My lips brush the side of his face, the cords of his neck.

I come first, and a moment later, he shakes, pulling out as he spills all over me.

The shower washes it away.

By the time we dry off, it's late, but I'm nowhere near sleep. He's not either. He spies something on my shelf and raises a brow.

"Jerry bought me that for my birthday."

He unrolls the travel chess set, the pieces too small for his fingers.

Still, he's beating me from the first move.

"How did you get so good?" I murmur. "Did Jerry teach you?"

"No. Cross did. Before I saw him for the manipulator he is."

Some people are live wires. They need careful management so they don't burn out, or catch fire, or destroy themselves.

"You really think there's nothing good in him."

"What do you mean?"

"He didn't start Wicked to destroy young lives."

"Maybe he wanted money. Fame." Jax shrugs. "Power. Why?"

I understand what it's like to want something bigger than yourself.

"No reason." I feel Jax's gaze on me, but I focus on the board.

"Come on," I mutter, hitting the run key again and wrestling my lip with my teeth.

Code flashes on the screen. As I hold my breath, the solution appears.

Ninety percent.

After the last month of hard work, my program explains nine-tenths of why a song is a hit. What's more, it makes recommendations about what to change in the levels, frequency— hell, even the effects—to make it more appealing.

I sigh, relief and pleasure washing over me as I slump in my chair. I glance at the clock in the interns' office. I'm the only intern in IT this fall, and my stuff has spread out over the other desks.

But it's late enough nearly everyone's gone for the day.

Since everything that happened with Mace, I've realized being kicked out of school isn't as huge as I thought. It's not life or death. The rest —winning the competition or getting back into school—I'll figure it out.

If anything, I'm more determined than ever to do something that matters.

I reach into my pocket for the slip of paper with Jax's lyrics. It needs a starting point, musically speaking. Chords. A key. Maybe even a melody. If only he'd do that.

Then I could actually use my app. To take it to the next level.

Before I can get too excited, my phone rings with an incoming video call.

"Hey," I say when Jax's face appears. "You're in the house."

"Closed yesterday. I'm surrounded by boxes and takeout."

"I'm surprised you notice. It's ten thousand square feet." I shift the computer off my lap. "Did Mace arrive today?"

"In one piece and grumpy as fuck. Cast on his arm and leg. Had to get him a special bed." Jax's gaze looks past me. "Where are you?"

"Wicked."

His mouth tightens. "It's midnight."

"I'm working on my program."

"You can't do that at home?"

I shoot him a look.

He blows out a breath. "You coming for Thanksoween?"

"I thought it was Halloween."

"Nah. See, when we're on tour, we don't get much downtime for the holidays. Our October to December is basically the same as the rest of the year. So, we had to roll them all into one. 'Merry Thanksoween' involves tailgating off the bus with turkey and candy."

I can't help laughing at the visual. "Right. Presents?"

Jax grins too. "Does booze count?"

"Sure." It sounds like fun. "Then I guess if it's a tour tradition, everyone on tour should come. Lita, Kyle, Brick." He curses. "That doesn't sound like Thanksoween spirit," I tease him.

"It's been a rough month."

"True. But all the more reason, Jax." I shift in

my seat. "If need be, I will *personally* get you in the mood."

He tosses the hair out of his face, glancing past the camera. "I'm in a public place, but give me two minutes…"

"I mean with snacks. Festive music," I chide. "Do you ever *not* think about sex?"

"If it's a toss-up between the "Monster Mash" and sex, I'll take sex. Every time."

I'm pretty sure I'm the luckiest girl in the world. Because the sex Jax Jamieson is talking about?

Yeah. It's with me.

In his bed. In my shower. In my bed.

He suggested we do it next to my poster of him, but I shot him down.

I think he was joking.

I hope he was.

Although now that I think about it…

I shake my head. It feels like we've only scratched the surface. I can tell from the way he looks at me that he wants so much more.

I'm not sure I can keep up.

"I lived like a saint the last few years, Hales."

"Your own fault."

"Or maybe I was waiting for you."

The offhand comment hits me in the solar plexus.

Even though the days he stayed over when Mace was in hospital were hellish, I feel like they brought us closer.

Sure, he's still in Dallas, and I'm still in Philly.

He's a rock star—okay, recovering—and I'm a student—fine, not even. But I can't give up on the tiny glimmer of hope in my chest that maybe we're something special, like Jax himself.

"Get home safe, Hales." His voice pulls me back. "Text me when you get there."

I hang up and pack up my things. Maybe I'm projecting. Looking for someone to pluck me from obscurity, to tell me I mean something to them.

Since the night at the jazz concert, I haven't seen Cross once.

I know he's the head of a company, and I rarely saw him before, but now I have the feeling he's keeping me at arm's length.

I go to pick up my mail on the way out. There's an envelope there, and it doesn't look like a paycheck.

I open it carefully, my breath catching when I get to the end.

It's an employment offer to work in the tech department next semester.

Full-time.

This has to be Cross's doing, but I have zero idea why he did it. Because they need help? Or as a favor?

Maybe he wants to see you more.

I'm not sure what to make of that, but I want to find out.

Cross probably isn't here, but I take the stairs up to the third floor just in case.

As I start down the dark hallway, I notice lights on in the recording studio. The door's open a crack.

I peer through the door, through the dark mixing booth, to the bright studio beyond.

There's a teenager in there. She doesn't look like the usual commercial type.

The girl finishes, and a familiar voice comes over the mic. "Try it from the bridge. We'll get what we can in the next few minutes. I don't want to keep people waiting."

My chest tightens as I take in the silhouette in front of the single lit computer screen.

I slide out of view, flattening my back against

the wall. Is this why Cross said there was no studio time? He's recording kids?

Maybe this is how he finds them. His new recruiting strategy. The age of reality TV and YouTube stars is saturated, so he's going back to first principles—recruiting from local talent.

Maybe you should leave before you land yourself in an epic amount of trouble. From what I've seen, getting on Cross's bad side is not a good idea.

On my way out, I see three more high school students walk in the front doors. I expect security to send them packing, but the guard on duty waves them through.

I can't resist stopping one of them, a kid who can't be more than fourteen, with full lips and spiked hair.

"They're running a few minutes late," I offer. He mutters a thanks, but I continue. "Are there more of you coming? Or is this it for tonight?"

He hesitates, glancing down at the badge on my hip. The credibility seems to soothe him a little. "I think we're the last slot."

His voice sends ripples down my spine, and I know he can sing. "Your parents don't notice you coming home this late?"

He smiles. "My parents can't keep track of themselves."

"Right." I match his smile, though I don't feel it on the inside.

"Tyler!" one of the other kids calls from the elevator. "Come on."

"It was nice meeting you," I say.

"Yeah, sure." He gives me a strange look, but the smile lingers.

"Hey, Tyler!" I call as the doors are about to close. They open again, one of the kids muttering under his breath. "Did you have to audition for this?"

"No. You just sign up at school and get on the wait list." He cocks his head. "Only thing I ever signed up for, I think."

The doors close, and I'm left in the dark.

16

"Where do you put this?"

Mace looks up from his iPad as I squint at the bird on the island. The package of stuffing is next to it. "Inside."

"Inside where?"

"You know." Mace makes a circle with the fingers of one hand and plunges the other through it. "Inside."

I shoot him a dirty look.

"You never made a turkey before, Jamieson?"

"Do I look like I've made a fucking turkey before?" Every bit of attention I can muster is on the turkey lying legs-up in the big foil pan. "Why are we doing this?"

"Because you told your girlfriend about our little tailgating tradition, and she did what girlfriends do and made it less weird."

I take the stuffing and start... well... stuffing it.

"You're seriously not going to respond to that?"

"And say what? That she's not my girlfriend? Call her whatever you want." He stares at me in stunned silence. "Better yet, take a fucking picture."

A few months ago, the idea of dating someone would've seemed insane. But recently, I've realized I'm slightly obsessed with Haley.

Not just physically. Hanging out with her. Hearing about her day. Finding out what riles her up. Comparing notes about TV and new albums and everything under the sun.

We used to talk once or twice a week. Since Mace's little hospital visit, it's nearly every day.

A fact that probably hasn't escaped her and sure as hell doesn't escape me.

A tritone sounds, and I turn to glance at my phone on the counter behind me.

.   .   .

Haley: Just landed. On our way. I have good news and bad news.

When I turn back, Mace is watching me.

"Still can't believe you ditched the flip phone."

"It was time."

With a screen and full keyboard, I can call and text her without it taking an hour to ask a simple question.

Plus, emojis.

You can get really dirty with emojis.

But impromptu eggplants aren't enough to satisfy me.

The past few days, an idea's been forming.

Haley's been busting her ass on this app, and if it's anywhere near as good as I think it is, she has a career in front of her.

If she's not in school, there's nothing keeping her in Philly. She could work on her app anywhere.

In theory.

I go back to the turkey, and my lip curls. It feels like penance.

"Wouldn't kill you to help," I say.

His brows rise as he lifts his chin to better meet my gaze over the counter from his wheelchair. Technically, he could be on crutches, but the doctors suggested this was easier given the nature of his breaks. "It might."

I go back to the bird. "All the more reason," I mutter.

The house closed on Wednesday, and a company I hired through my agent moved my shit here. Mace came on his own.

In the couple of days since, we've binge-watched three seasons of sci-fi shows, drank a lot of beer—hard liquor is off the table given the meds he's on, which I insisted he take if he's going to stay with me—and basically acted like kids.

What we haven't done is talk about what happened.

I finish filling the bird with bread and wash my hands with extra soap, turning back to him.

"Stepping off a building is pretty fucking drastic, Ryan." I can't remember the last time I called him that, and from the expression on his face, he can't either.

He blows out a breath, shaking his head and

shooting me a look of supreme disappointment. "We're going to do this now?"

"Yeah. We're going to do this now." He stares at me, but I'm not done. "You think I don't get you. That I haven't been there."

He rubs his good hand over his jaw. Or I think he does, because he's rocking a *Cast Away* beard. "You haven't."

I go to the bar, start hauling bottles out for tonight. "I saved your ass. Every time touring spun you out, I pulled you back."

I unscrew the top of the bourbon and pour one for myself. The smoky flavor burns my throat as I meet my friend's somber gaze.

"It's different for you. You're Cross's fucking boy wonder—you were from the start. Everyone wanted a piece of you."

"That's crap." I don't for a second believe this is about jealousy. He's been in this business too long, been on too many stages, cashed too many checks. "You've been part of Riot Act since the beginning. You know how this works. You're on top until someone takes a swipe at you. Until the world decides you're too big and cuts you off at the knees."

"That's the stupid part, Jax. You cut yourself

off at the knees," he mutters. "You're on top of the damn universe, and instead of riding the ride, you stepped off."

Anger rises inside me, but he's not done. Under the facial hair, his blue eyes flash.

"You're quitting because what—you want to make amends? The rest of us sit around because we can't do what you want to. If we had half the chances you have, we'd be doing every one of those things. Trust me on that."

I hate hearing him talk like this because even if the words aren't true, they're true for him. He believes them.

We've been friends as long as I've been at this. He's the closest thing I have to a brother. And what burns me is I didn't know.

He didn't tell me what was going on. I wasn't there to see him. To chew him out.

To fix him.

The doorbell rings. Or more accurately, the security bell for the front gate.

I hit the buzzer to admit the car.

"You have good Thanksgivings growing up, Ry?"

"No."

"Me either. But let's fucking pretend for one night."

We finish in the kitchen, and a few minutes later, I hear the front door open. The beeping of the disabled alarm system.

"Jamieson!"

I'd know Lita's call anywhere, and I stride through the hallway, my socks padding on the marble as they come into view.

Lita's wearing some purple dress that makes her bright-red hair even redder as she drops the overnight bag next to her. Brick slides in after her, and Kyle too. They seem to have borne the brunt of the luggage. Serena sets a suspicious-looking carrier in front of her as she steps out of tall heels.

My gaze narrows. "Tell me you didn't bring that thing to my house."

"He can't fend for himself for a weekend."

I bend and inspect the bars, the little nose poking through. I shake my head.

"We didn't think they'd let her take him on the plane," Lita says. "But she dyed him black and convinced them he was a cat."

I glance up as one more comes through the door.

I swear the front hall gets a little brighter.

Haley's wearing a dress that stops halfway down her thighs with tights and these tiny boots. Her cheeks are flushed, her lips curved.

She drops her bag and crosses to me, glancing toward the carrier on the way. "That's the bad news. Sorry." She leans in so we're sharing breath, and I'm hypnotized by the sheen of her lip gloss as she lowers her voice. "We'll wait until she's asleep, then put him in the garage. You want to hear the good news?"

I drop my mouth to hers and feel her surprised intake of breath as I kiss her.

The chuckles and comments in the background barely register.

Haley's body melts under my hands, and when I pull back, her lips are soft.

"You're the good news, Hales."

The smile on her face takes the edge off everything.

That's when I know it's true.

I'm totally falling for this girl.

I'd expected careening headfirst for someone would be accompanied with dread.

But now that I'm admitting it, it's not. It's like a weight has lifted off me.

Haley tilts her head, her gaze working over mine. "What is it?"

I grin. "Nothing."

As much as I'd like to stay in this bubble, we've got a Thanksoween to deliver.

I link my fingers through hers and tug her after me to find the others.

When we walk into the kitchen, Lita has her arms around Mace's neck, and he's a few shades darker than I remember.

She turns her attention toward the counter. "Ooh, I love it when men cook."

"You know that needs at least four hours, right?" Serena says.

"Was just about to put it in, Skunk Girl." I fold my arms over my chest. "We have twenty years on international tours filling stadiums. I think we can cook a damned turkey."

"Did you take out the giblets?"

"The what?" Mace and I echo.

We spend the rest of the day drinking and cooking and talking.

Then we finally sit down to dinner. It's the

only time I can see using my formal dining room, and the table I had delivered yesterday works like a charm.

"Since this is a Halloween and Thanksgiving hybrid, should we say what we're thankful for?" Serena quips over the gravy.

"Wrapping albums," Lita says.

Serena says, "Old friends. And new ones."

"Good food," Kyle says.

"Hard pass," says Mace, and I shoot him a look.

"Things working out," Haley says. "I may not be in school, but I can pay the rent and program. I submitted my app to the competition yesterday."

Pride fills my chest as everyone congratulates her, as if I had some part in it.

In a way, I did.

"What about Wicked?" Lita asks.

Haley's gaze meets mine, and I swear there's guilt in it. "I was offered a chance to stay on in the IT department. I'm thinking through it."

That comment has me dropping the spoon back in the cranberry sauce. "I thought you owed Cross four months, then you were done with it."

"Maybe I want to stay."

Everyone turns to me.

"What about you, Jax?" Lita asks, clearly sensing the tension.

"You could start with this big-ass house," Serena says.

"Or the fact that you make music that makes girls strip naked," Kyle offers.

"Think I hear something buzzing," I mutter, rising from my seat and turning toward the kitchen. A chorus of boos follows.

"I didn't mean it!" Kyle hollers.

The rest of dinner gets monopolized by Lita recounting stories from Nashville, which Haley sometimes jumps in on, and Serena answering Kyle's questions about her skunk. Including how he escapes everything.

"That better not include his damned cage," I mutter as I'm having seconds of potatoes.

Serena's answer is to gulp more wine.

But I couldn't care less about the skunk because I'm still stuck on what Haley said.

Wicked offered her a job, and she's thinking of taking it.

Just when I thought he'd finished screwing with my life.

He can't know I'm thinking of asking her to move in with me. I know that logically.

But more than that, it bugs me that she's thinking about it. That she wants anything to do with the guy after what he's done to both of us.

After we all eat way too much dinner, we move to the massive living room overlooking the patio to drink and eat candy. The pool's heated, but no one wants to swim. Lita and Brick play the requisite game of *Guitar Hero*. Mace and Haley place bets on the outcome.

Serena's gone to take the little demon for a walk. Kyle tags along, asking something about skunk charities when their voices are cut off by the closing front door.

I'm drinking and ignoring the game.

At least until my glass is empty.

I get up and go to the kitchen to refill it.

"So what are other traditions of Thanksoween?"

Haley's low voice has me looking over my shoulder.

The tights should keep me from thinking about her legs wrapped around me, but nope. Her dress has little points of sleeves and neckline that's a modest curve, but I'm jealous of the fact that it's touching her all over and I'm not.

"After dessert and drinks, the guests blow the host."

She shifts a hip against the marble island, raising a brow. "All the guests? I'm not sure I can compete with Kyle. He has that raw enthusiasm going for him."

I shake my head, turning back to pour another bourbon.

"How's Annie?" she asks after a moment.

"She won't talk to me."

Haley makes a face, reaching for her stomach. "I'm sorry, Jax. I know it doesn't feel like it now, but she'll come around. She'll see how much you care about her and that you only want what's best for her."

"Maybe. In the meantime, the lawyers can deal with it." Haley's questioning look makes me go on. "Annie knows who I am now. There's already a confirmation of paternity, thanks to her mother. So there's nothing stopping me filing for custody."

She looks stunned. "You're going to sue for access? Jax, she's been given some information that's turned her life upside down. She needs time."

"A month? Two? I guess that's what it took for you to forgive the man who ignored you your whole life and go to work for him."

I know I'm being an asshole about this, but I can't seem to let it go.

Haley lifts her chin, and the light catches her hair. The hair she put up in some kind of style, maybe for her, but maybe—just a little—for me. "Jax. I was going to tell you about that. It just came up," she says under her breath. "But I'm not turning my back on Wicked just because you have."

She looks like she's about to say more, but in the end, she walks out of the kitchen without another word.

17

Jax's stubble comes in redder than the rest of his hair.

I never noticed since we've only shared a bed a handful of times. But when I wake up in the four-poster bed next to him, it catches the light.

I take a second to enjoy looking at him. Not only because he looks gorgeous lying on the king mattress, the covers drifting down around his abs in a way that's completely distracting, but because he looks peaceful.

As if, for once, he's not fighting the world.

We can forgive a child who is afraid of the dark. The tragedy is when men are afraid of the light.

The quote comes back to me. I think it's Plato, but I'm not sure.

I feel closer to Jax than I've ever felt to another person. Since Mace's hospital visit, it's as if his walls have come down even more. I feel it in the way he talks to me, the way he looks at me.

But I'm not sure what to do with what I find on the other side of those walls. Jax seems to be in a tug-of-war with the world. I feel it even when he smiles. Even when we're together.

Serena asked me on the plane yesterday if I'm falling in love with Jax.

I told her no because in some ways, I've always loved him. When I knew every word to every song he wrote, I loved him.

But that's fan love, the way you love anything that's too perfect.

He's not perfect. He's strong and flawed and beautiful and wrong. He hates me working at Wicked, and it's driving a wedge between us.

But I love the way his amber eyes glow when he's thinking dirty thoughts or laughing at me when I nerd out on him. I love his obsession with reality TV, especially the home reno shows, and the fact that he can name every kind of power tool known to man even though he's never used one. I love how responsible he feels for his family, his friends, even when it strains him.

I shift out of bed and grab one of the two robes on the back of the door.

The smaller one is so soft and fluffy I suck in a breath.

It fits me perfectly.

That's what reminds me good things take time. When he does something like that.

The huge house is quiet except for Kyle's snoring coming through an open door. I make my way downstairs, my feet sinking into the plush carpet.

My phone's in my purse, where I left it last night. There's a missed call from Cross's assistant, but the battery's nearly dead and it's a Sunday. Rather than calling her back, I move the phone to the wireless charging pad in the kitchen.

Maybe she was returning my call about the "after school program."

I tried to arrange a meeting with Cross, but she told me he was out of the office for the rest of the week.

So I pieced some of it together myself from cryptic notations on studio calendars.

The nearest I can figure is Cross makes the studio's time, his time, available as some kind of charitable act. The strange part is there's no PR, no media or public announcements.

Which means he doesn't want anyone to know.

Because he's doing something wrong, or because he doesn't want to be rewarded for doing something right?

It's confusing, and as much as I'd like to tell someone, I can't talk to Jax about this. He wouldn't believe Cross would do anything for someone other than himself.

I don't feel much like eating, thanks to the big meal last night. But the coffee maker beckons in all its chrome glory.

It's way more advanced than what's at the café, but I figure it out in no time. I press a few of the buttons, and it starts whirring, grinding beans at a deafening volume that's sure to wake everyone in this house.

I yank the cord from the wall until the quiet resumes.

Later.

I go to the back patio and watch the sun rising over the distant hills.

I feel him behind me before his hands find my shoulders.

"You're up early." Jax's voice at my ear is a low rumble, as sexy as the first time I heard it.

My smile starts inside me, unfolding like a flower. The fact that I don't jump when I feel him close, even when he surprises me, shows how much has changed. "I heard a sound. Maybe the house spawned another bedroom overnight."

His chuckle tickles my skin. "Come back to bed."

I place a hand over his and turn toward him. He's wearing pajama pants slung low on his hips, and his chest is a delicious map of muscle and ink and beautiful skin. "Anyone else awake?"

Jax shakes his head, his hand caressing my cheek.

I can tell the moment affection slides into more.

He slips a hand inside the front of my robe as he kisses me, lightly at first. Then he pulls me back with him toward the house. Turns and presses me against it. My breath catches. He hitches my leg up around his hip, and the pajama pants do nothing to hide the growing hardness between us.

I want to resist, because it shouldn't be this easy. But on some level, I crave it.

His mouth grazes mine. Lazy and assured. His fingers brush my breast, teasing my nipple in the cold morning air until it's even harder.

"What are you doing?" I manage.

"Saying good morning."

Even if my head wanted to stop him, my body craves him.

His hand strokes lower, fighting with the tie on my robe. Winning, like he usually does.

"Mmm. Good mornings start with coffee."

"I promise this will wake you up."

He brushes between my legs. My head falls back against the side of the house, my hair catching on the brick.

He's patient and insistent, as though this is an inevitability.

Maybe it is.

Jax touches me, a few deliberate strokes as he watches my expression, then presses inside. He swallows my moan, soothes my tension with his tongue and spirals it tighter at once.

I tear my lips from his, scraping my teeth along his jaw.

It takes a few minutes, a few strokes, until I

come, moaning his name into the tendons of his neck.

After, we go inside and he turns on the coffee, oblivious to the deafening noise.

I cross to his fridge.

"Nice calendar," I call over the sound.

"I like it. I like paper. Not having everything online."

The whirring stops, and the brew cycle, mercifully, starts. My gaze scans the rows of days. "What's that?" I point at an entry.

"Car commercial."

"For real?"

He shoots me a quelling look. "Got to keep the money flowing."

I know firsthand what it's like to be worried about cash, but I can't imagine Jax having that same concern.

Maybe it never goes away.

"You ever think you'd have more fun doing something musical?"

He raises a brow.

"When was the last time you picked up a guitar? You could go on YouTube again, do more acoustic sessions. Or teach kids who are into music."

"You sound like my agent. He keeps feeding me shit about my brand." Jax pulls the coffee cup from under the machine, holding it out to me. I smell it.

"Whoa. That's good."

"I've got some skills, Hales." His gaze twinkles.

"I'm serious. But you don't have to do it for your brand. Or anyone. Do it for you."

He reaches for a water glass, fills and drains it without breaking eye contact. "I need to show you something."

He walks me through the halls, flicking on lights as we go to the garage at the side of the house.

He hits a master switch that illuminates the cavernous space.

My jaw drops.

It's filled with guitars, boxes, bagged clothes, and posters stacked ten deep.

"Jax, this is a fortune worth of equipment and memorabilia..."

"Trust me, I remember all of it." His face hardens as he points at a framed poster. "This was New Orleans. From our second tour. Mace overdosed, and I held him in the streets until the ambulance came and brought him back." He lifts a guitar. "Wicked bought me this when I refused to sign the contract. It's signed by Springsteen. When I got the guitar and picked it up for the first time, Annie's mother left her with Grace."

In the corner is a gold statue, and Jax lifts it. "This is a Grammy. For the first album I cut, about the life I left behind." He straightens, his gaze hard on mine. "I meant what I said last night. That chapter is closed."

"But it's not a chapter, Jax. It's a limb. How can you cut that part of you off?" I think of the kids I watched recording with Cross. If he was anything like them, I can understand how Cross was drawn to him. "You're so bright. You matter so much to so many people."

"I never asked to," he says softly. "Some people think fame's one-sided. It's not. It's a give and take because without fans, you have nothing. I'm grateful for them. They've given me a chance to make music. To see the world. To do things my parents would've never dreamed.

"But sometimes the pull is so strong. What they want exceeds what you can give.

"I need to get my family back together, Hales, and if I need to fight for them, I will. I'm not waiting until Annie's grown up. Until she's obsessed with makeup and boys and has the option to ignore me."

I've never heard Jax talk this way before, and I can't help but be affected.

"I get it. At least, I think I do. Though I don't know many twenty-nine-year-old guys who'd turn their backs on being famous to fight for their daughter."

He takes hold of my hips, and I dig my fingers into his forearms. "I hope you don't know many twenty-nine-year-old guys. I like having you to myself."

His eyes darken, and already I'm breathless just being near him. The sound of his voice and the feel of his hands wrapping around me like silk.

"Move in with me."

I'm having trouble hearing. And as a side effect, breathing.

"Wait, what?"

"I'm serious, Hales." A ghost of a smile flickers across his handsome face. "You're out of school. My roommate situation is temporary. I don't know what life looks like after music, but I'll figure it out."

Apparently my hearing is fine. It's my processing that's fucked up. Because I can't make sense of the words he's uttering.

"I'm happy when you're with me," he goes on, his amber gaze running over my face. "It's simple. The simplest thing I've ever known. I love how I can tell you anything and you don't judge me. You don't want anything from me. You don't care if my house has four bedrooms or forty, but it's not because you don't know my world. You've seen it firsthand. You get it. Hell, you've been on that stage, Hales. And after all of it, you want *me*."

Stringing words together coherently is impossible, so I just stare at him. His hair is falling over his face at the front, and I do the one thing I can in this moment and reach up to brush it away.

The idea of living in this house is beyond insane, but getting to be with Jax every day, touching him, waking up next to him, laughing with him? It's a damned fantasy.

Because you're so in love with him you can't think of anything else.

It's true. I realize it's true even as he says, "You're hesitating. Why?"

The easy confidence he always projects wavers for the first time.

"I feel the same way," I manage. "With the happy and the simple... And I can't believe I'm saying this, because part of me just wants to say yes and kiss you, but the biggest thing is sometimes I feel like you're humoring me."

"How so?"

"You're older, experienced. I can't even get oral sex without freaking out." I raise a brow. "Unless maybe that's the plan. You've been secretly looking for a woman you can avoid going down on for all time. In which case, you've definitely found her."

His look of shock dissolves into an admiring grin. "That's not why I like you, Hales. I like how you care about people. I like that you speak your mind. I like that you take things at face value instead of looking for darkness in the world. And as for me going down on you? I'm thinking of that as a long-term project." He leans in, his lips grazing my jaw and making me arch into his kiss. "One I will work at for as long as it takes to get the job done."

Oh, God. I'm ready to sign away my life to be

hammered, nailed, and screwed by this man for all time.

I squeeze my eyes shut. A million thoughts bubble up inside me, all of them saying different things. Reasons for and against, questions, and more.

When I blink, taking in the sight of Jax Jamieson in front of me, every other thought falls away.

This is the man who makes the songs I live my life by. Who loves his daughter more than any father I know. Who I can't imagine being without.

Jax clears his throat. "I understand if you need time to—"

"No," I interrupt.

"No."

"I mean, yes," I say, and his face goes blank. "Yes, I want to."

His expression dissolves into a grin, and I don't know which one of us looks happier in this moment.

Scratch that. It has to be me. Because I can't imagine feeling any more joy than what's coursing through my body.

I shift onto my toes, grabbing him to press a

kiss to his mouth. His arms band around me as he returns the kiss, groaning against my mouth in a way that has me wet again.

"Haley! Jax!"

We groan in unison. But the panicked voices don't stop calling, and we go back inside.

The kitchen is full of somber faces.

"What is it?" Jax asks.

I'm already grabbing the phone from Lita's hand.

The headline on the news article has my smile and laughter falling away.

"Pioneering Music Executive Shannon Cross Dead at Fifty-Five"

Ice fills my body. My chest, my stomach, my lungs, my legs. "No."

"Haley."

I grab my phone and return the assistant's call, putting it on speaker. "What happened?"

"Haley. He passed last night. He had brain cancer, a quick-moving kind. He learned six months ago. He didn't want to treat it."

Disbelief tints everything, turning the room fuzzy. "It's not possible. I saw him last week, and..."

"He's been struggling for some time but didn't want to let on. I want to give you time, but we also need to plan."

"Excuse me?"

"He didn't want to burden you, so arrangements have been made. But as his next of kin, you should review his plans for the funeral."

"Review his..." I can't think.

"We'll call you back," Jax interrupts, his voice cutting short any argument. "We need a minute."

"Mr. Jamieson? Of course. Please don't wait too long. The hospital—"

"We won't."

18

"We nearly done here?" I shoot a look at my agent, who looks up from his phone.

The director nods. "Just a few more takes."

I swallow my frustration, reminding myself what I'm getting paid for this photo shoot.

I tried to convince Haley to stay until the funeral, but she said she needed to go back and help. The shock of Cross's death has hit everyone hard. My agent's getting calls every day from media, and for once, it's not to talk about me.

I turn them all down.

The only person who matters is her.

I asked her to move in with me last weekend,

and she said yes. But we haven't talked about it since.

Still, I'm hoping it's the change she needs after all this shit with Wicked. She can start fresh here. Build her own computer company if she wants to. If she doesn't, that's fine too.

My phone rings, and the number on the call display has my stomach hardening.

"You have some nerve, Jax Jamieson," Grace snaps in my ear.

"I told you I want her back."

"So you're suing for custody?" She's livid, and I get why. "We could work through access issues. But you don't just want to see her. You want a court to say you get her half the time."

I want her all the time, but saying that won't help. For now, I don't want to take any chance of Grace packing Annie up and taking her away from me. And I want Grace's prick of a husband to know I'm watching and I have recourse if he fucks up.

Her heavy breathing fills my ear. "When we were kids and someone picked on me at school, you told him not to fuck with us. But what you meant was don't fuck with *you*. You can't stand someone telling you you can't have what you want. Can't *do* what you want. You never got over that, did you, big brother?" She curses. "I can't believe you're doing this to her."

I think of Haley, without a father her whole life, and now that she finds him, he's gone. "I'm not doing this to her. I'm doing it *for* her."

I hit End before she can respond.

19

HALEY

There are a lot of moving parts to a funeral. But the funeral of Shannon Cross is on a whole other scale.

First, lots of people knew my father.

My father.

Two, no one knew he was sick.

Now everyone wants to talk, and since the juicy bit of info that I'm his daughter seems to have leaked? The person they want to talk to is me.

Serena's been glued to my side all week at Wicked as I make arrangements, working with Cross's assistant.

I keep it together, accepting condolences and making decisions. Though really, he had most of it figured out. Speakers. Invitations. The drinks at his visitation. Hell, even the flowers.

I didn't peg Shannon Cross as a flower guy.

That's the part I want to scream when people shoot me looks of sympathy and pity or ask what he would have wanted.

I don't know him. And I never will.

"It's a lot of people," I say, looking out the window of the limo past Jax.

"It's the end of an era. Wicked Records has ruled for decades."

I've never seen Jax in a suit, and he's so handsome I wish I could appreciate it more. Clean-shaven with a dark suit, crisp shirt, and no tattoos in sight, he could be a record executive himself.

The only hint of rock star about him—besides the fact that he's the most gorgeous man I've ever seen—is the way his hair falls over his forehead at the front.

Jax's strong fingers thread through mine, and I stare at them. He's not usually a PDA kind of guy, and after the hellish week, the move touches me more than I could've imagined.

"Thanks for coming."

"My agent would have my hide if I didn't." He

forces a smile. "But I'm not here for him. I'm here for you, Hales. And I'm not going anywhere."

A warm feeling starts in my stomach, spreads through my body.

He can't possibly appreciate what it means to hear that, but knowing Jax Jamieson has my back makes everything else a little better.

And he's mine. He asked me to move in with him and I said yes. Even if we haven't talked about it since, I know we will.

"What will happen to Wicked?" I ask under my breath.

"What do you think?"

I hesitate. "I don't know. I've spent all week thinking about the man; there's been no time to think about the company. I guess someone else will take it over."

He shrugs. "Or it could be sold off to pay for expenses. Those artists on contract will be released. Some people will get their money out, others won't."

"You mean it could be over?"

"Yeah."

My stomach clenches. Something about that feels wrong.

More wrong than the fact that Wicked's

founder, its leader, is lying in a casket a few hundred feet away.

On TV, it always rains at funerals, but today is sunny. A ton of people are gathered around the cemetery.

My eye lands on a girl my age with straight platinum-blond hair that glows against her black dress.

I spoke with Ariel on the phone once this week to let her know about the arrangements, to see if her family would come.

She's with her father, who doesn't look so different from mine. They should look alike since they're brothers.

Jax and I stand in the front row. I'm in a daze as the minister speaks. When people cover the casket in roses.

"Miss Cross? Would you like to say a few words?"

It's Telfer.

Of course, I don't say it.

I reach for the folded paper in my pocket and walk toward the front.

The people in the crowd blur together as a lump rises in my throat.

I've done speaking before. I had help

preparing for today from people who knew him better than I did.

Pretty much everyone.

When my mom died, I went to see a counsellor who told me there were a lot of things I might feel. Overwhelm. Grief.

Guilt.

This is different but not easier.

I open my mouth to start the speech I wrote and rewrote, but nothing comes out.

The birds in the trees don't share my affliction, chirping in the background like it's any other day.

My gaze finds Jax in the front row. He's the last person to mourn Shannon Cross, but here he is.

Jax's dark head inclines. So slight it's nearly imperceptible.

I've never asked for a savior before, but now I can't move. I want to tell him I'm frozen.

With my eyes, I try.

In the space of a breath, he's unclasped his hands and he's at my side. His dress shoes toe the damp grass next to mine, and I feel taller and braver at once.

I wait for him to speak.

He doesn't.

We stand there in a beam of cold sunlight, wrapped in our coats and hats, as Jax Jamieson sings the first cover I've ever heard him perform.

Leonard Cohen's "Hallelujah" fills the cemetery, disappearing at the edges into the crisp winter air.

There are no walls to reflect the sound, to warm it, to capture it. There is just the crowd and the trees whose leaves have fallen and the most beautiful voice I've ever heard.

"That was something else." Lita follows the direction of my stare as we stand together inside the reception hall.

"It might be the last time he sings in public."

"That'd be a crime." She pours a drink. "Did I ever tell you I was going to be a veterinarian?"

"No. For real?"

"Yup. I had straight A's in high school. Got accepted to a good college. But I got the chance to book a tour and I never looked back. Now I have a rented apartment, no car."

"You regret it?"

"Never." She takes a long sip. "When people don't do what they're meant to do, it eats at them. You saw Mace. Being told he's not needed anymore's like telling him he's living in a cage. Even Jerry can't stop because he doesn't know any other way."

"Jax isn't like that."

"No. For Jax, it'll be worse." Her words make me straighten. "He just won't realize it until it's too late." She downs the rest of the drink.

I watch her go as a man in a suit winds his way toward me.

"Excuse me, Miss Cross."

"Telfer," I say.

I've heard the name dozens of times this week. Hundreds.

It's felt petty to correct people under the circumstances, but now I need to remind the world I'm not Haley Cross. I have an identity that has nothing to do with a man I never met until this summer.

"Miss Telfer. I was your father's lawyer. I need to talk to you about his will. With his other surviving family."

He pulls me into a room where the other

family's already waiting and delivers what he has to say.

Each phrase of legal jargon streams in one ear, out the other. But when he gets to the punch line, I ask him to repeat it.

Twice.

"There you are." Serena's worried eyes leap out from below the black fascinator pinned in her hair as I emerge from the room. "I've been looking for you for ages. What was that about?"

"He left me everything." Serena's eyes widen, but I can't feel anything except numbness seeping through me. "His money. His house."

She rubs my arm. "Okay. Well, that's understandable."

I press a hand to my face. "Serena, he left me his *company*."

I hear her gasp, but I'm looking past her to where Jax is talking with someone across the room. As if sensing me, he turns, a questioning look on his handsome face.

"I own Wicked."

"Any word from the lawyers?" I ask Jax as he drops into the seat across from me at the campus café.

It's quiet in the morning, with most students either still asleep or in class. The familiarity of it all—the tables, the chairs, the stage area—is much needed after the chaos of the last week and a half.

"The petition for custody's gone in. Grace's lawyer's responded that they're contesting it."

The tightness in Jax's voice reminds me he hasn't had a walk in the park lately either.

I reach across the table to weave my fingers through his.

"When are you going back to Dallas?"

"Tomorrow."

He stayed at a hotel last night because he and Scrunchie have decided the apartment isn't big enough for two alpha males.

"Come with me, Hales." His amber eyes fill with determination. "Pack a bag and come. Serena can bring the rest of your things, or you can get them later. Hell, we don't even have to go to Dallas right away; we can take a vacation on a beach somewhere. You and me and some peanut-free island we can get lost in."

I want to scream yes because the one thing that hasn't changed is how much I care about him. Through all of this, he's been there for me. Although I'm not sure life will ever feel normal again, I want to pretend it can.

I want to order some pizza and watch home reno shows and documentaries with the rock star I'm completely in love with. I want to shut the door on the world and just pretend *forever*.

"I want to, Jax. You have no idea how much." He leans in, and there's so much satisfaction in his expression I want to purr. "But I have to tell you something. Cross left me Wicked."

The tension invading his body is a living

thing, and I wonder if he even notices the way he straightens in his chair.

"*Shit.*"

"I met with the lawyers this morning. They said I could look for an investor to buy it or to sell it off for parts."

Jax's jaw works. "What are you thinking?"

I tell him what I spent the morning deciding. "I'm not doing either."

His touch is gone as he folds his arms over his chest, pulling the long-sleeved shirt across his biceps. "What do you mean?"

I remember finding the kids recording late at night. There's so much I need to know. If not about Shannon Cross, then about the work he did.

"He left me his legacy, Jax. He's built something that matters. Maybe I don't fully understand it yet, and maybe he lost himself in the building of it. But he's made it possible to create music that changes the world, and changes the people who made it. I won't turn my back on it, or take it apart. Not yet."

I need him to understand this.

Judging by the way he shifts his chair back, it's not going well.

The satisfaction is long gone from his face, replaced by wariness and accusation.

"If you pulled back any further you'd be at another table right now." I mean it as a joke, but it's an observation.

"You're keeping the company," he says at last.

"Yes."

"And you'll stay here and run it?"

I know it must sound ridiculous. "I'll leave people in charge who know what they're doing. But I want to be part of it."

"You're not coming back to Dallas."

The hurt in his voice twists my gut.

"It's not the right time." I lean forward, trying to close the space between us. "We can fly back and forth. Or you could come to Philly."

"I'm fighting for my daughter, Hales," he mutters. "I can't do that from another city."

My heart squeezes. "Jax, nothing else has to change."

"Everything's changing," he insists, his voice raw. "You don't even know him—you don't even like him. But you're choosing him."

"I'm not choosing him. I..." My throat works as I try to come up with words that will make this right. "I need to *understand* him."

If anyone knows what it's like to have a family in chaos, to want to put things right, it's Jax.

He rubs a hand over his jaw, and I'm praying he's starting to get it.

At least until he says, "I'm not living my life at Shannon Cross's whim, especially now that he's dead. If you do this, we're done."

Done.

It's such a good thing, being done. All my life I've taken pride in getting through.

Through my mom's death, through tour, through more coding all-nighters than I can count.

This kind of done grabs me like a fist.

I remember our conversation in the back of a Town Car outside a bowling alley in Dallas on a warm summer night.

You're standing on the edge of a cliff, looking down into the abyss, and you're twice afraid.

Once for the knowledge that you could fall and perish.

And once for the knowledge that the choice of whether to stay or whether to jump is ultimately yours.

"I signed the papers this morning."

My whispered words hang between us like the ice on the trees outside.

All of it feels like years ago. The bowling alley, our kiss on his bus. The day I showed up at his hotel and he took me apart and put me back together again.

Jax's jaw works as he stares past me, unseeing, for a long moment.

I want to shake him, to tell him he's making this harder than it needs to be. That everything can be simple, even if it's not the way we'd planned.

Before I can, he rises from his chair and shifts over me, dropping a soft kiss on the top of my head. "I'll see you around, Hales," he murmurs against my hair.

But there's a finality that doesn't match the words.

When Jax walks out, I swear he takes my heart with him.

I look down at my hands tucked under the table. The drop of blood on my thumb where the nail's ripped.

I never got it before. What it means to exercise your ability to choose.

It's as if the whole world is crumbling from

the outside, falling in on itself. Burying you in a landslide.

Still, under the pressure and heaviness and pain and anxiety, I feel the tiniest shred of something burning inside my chest.

Purpose.

"Are you okay?" a voice asks from somewhere above me.

I blink up at one of the employees, a girl who's stopped next to the table. "I'm going to be fine," I say.

"Oh. I meant do you want another drink," she prompts, nodding to the empty glass in front of me.

I shake my head and she returns to the counter.

I'm going to be fine, I repeat, conviction building in my gut.

Because today, and tomorrow, and the day after that? I'm going to do something that matters.

Even if the man I love hates me for it.

21

HALEY

TWO YEARS LATER

I'm bleeding.

It's eight forty-five, and my lip looks as if it was the final victim in a B slasher flick.

"That's what liner's for," Serena's disembodied voice chirps from the phone on the marble bathroom vanity.

"I want to look like a damn grown-up for this meeting."

"You do. *Watch where you're fucking going! This isn't the Autobahn!*"

"Stop driving and talking. It's making me

nervous." I wet a tissue and dab my lip. The plum color that was supposed to say "sophisticated" leaks more.

"It's Bluetooth. I'll be at your door in five. In the meantime, use some makeup remover."

She clicks off before I can tell her I don't have makeup remover.

Concealer it is. I stab it on with a finger, then take one final look in the mirror at my pencil skirt and blouse before dashing out of the upstairs bathroom and down the creaky staircase as fast as my heels will safely carry me.

In the formal dining room off the hall, I take a quick inventory—computer bag, files, makeup kit, plus the coffee that brewed automatically—and gather everything on the custom table as Serena's Range Rover pulls up at the curb of my tree-lined street.

I walk out the door. There are birds in this older neighborhood, and mature trees just starting to blossom in the spring.

"Tell me it's not that bad," I say as I slide into the car, armload of gear in tow.

Serena inspects my face. "Do you want to start the day off with lies?"

I set two travel mugs in the console cup holders.

"I love that the owner of a record company makes me coffee."

"Part owner. And I love that you stayed with me." I mean it, and her eyes glint a little before she turns back to the road. "You ever regret it?"

"What, sticking with your nerdy ass? Never."

We cross town in less than ten minutes, and Serena pulls into the Wicked lot.

"Morning, Miss Telfer. Miss Daniels."

"Morning, Jeff." I nod to security as we cross the lobby.

We ride the elevator up to the top floor.

"Haley," Derek, who used to be the VP of production and moved into the CEO role after my father's death, greets me as I enter the boardroom.

I take a seat across from the rest of the management team, Serena on my heels.

"Serena, you're joining us?" He raises a brow.

"She is."

Wicked's head of production, Todd, runs a judgmental eye over her. "I understand she joined the PR department when you took control of Wicked, but you stopped calling the shots when you sold the company."

"I sold eighty percent of the company. I'm the only owner who works here." *Without expecting a paycheck,* I add silently.

"Work here?" he scoffs. "You run an after-school program."

Derek cuts in smoothly before I can argue. "I trust you reviewed the financials. We have little slack. The music industry is changing fast, and we're losing traction."

Moving Derek into the CEO position after my father passed away had seemed like the best move. I still don't regret it, though sometimes I think he lets me out of things in deference to my father. The fact that I kept him.

The new head of production has none of those biases.

"Our junior artists will help carry this company into a new age," I point out.

"They're children," Todd protests. "We should be dropping the program, not investing in it. Free up studio space we can lease. Not to mention the equipment. Their sweaty little hands are taking up a few hundred thousand in instruments and gear."

I straighten in my chair. "You can't be serious."

"None of them are in a position to supplement this company's income," Derek says. "It's not that they're untalented, but they're kids without proper training, media coaching. Now, we've spoken to the majority shareholders, and they're in favor of cost-cutting measures. This shouldn't come as a surprise. Wicked is a business venture for them. They don't have the... affection for it that you do."

"We're not dropping the program." The words sound raw from my dry throat. "Can we take a coffee break?"

Derek shoves his hands in his pockets, and Todd lets out an annoyed sigh. "Sure," Derek offers.

I rise from my seat and top off my coffee from the carafe in the corner. I feel Derek's presence before I see him.

"Listen," he starts under his breath. "We talked about using the program as a PR exercise. Do features on some of the kids. Hell, maybe we can claim a tax write-off if we spin it right."

I picture the faces of the high school kids who come through the studio. Performing here gives them something structured, but more importantly, it gives them space to create.

"They're not charity cases, Derek. They're artists. My father got that when he started the program. We're not doing them a favor; they're doing us one."

I go back to the table, taking my seat. Derek follows.

Across the table, Serena raises a brow. I probably look like I'm about to murder someone.

Derek turns to the lawyer. "Let's talk about our stars. How goes the outreach regarding current contracts?"

"We've tried to reach Mr. Jamieson. Reminded his attorney he's under contract."

Jax's name makes me sit up straighter.

"Nothing?" Todd sounds exasperated. "I've worked with some divas, but this is ridiculous."

"He told us to take him to court."

"Then do that." Todd's not bothering to hide his irritation. "Or let's move the hell on, Derek. He's not a rock star anymore. He's a glorified car salesman."

Serena jumps in. "As the person who runs this label's social media and half our ad budget? Jax Jamieson is still the biggest rock star on the planet. He could turn this around by breathing on it. His fans haven't forgotten him." Her gaze flicks to me. "Even if he's forgotten them."

I swallow the lump that rises in my throat at the mention of his name. "Have you talked to him?"

"He won't answer calls or return them." Wicked's lawyer weighs in.

"I don't understand how you let him walk away in the first place," the production head mutters, looking around the table.

That's a story you would never understand.

It's been two years since I saw his handsome face, but in some ways it feels like ten.

In some ways, it feels like yesterday.

My fingers slide under the table, tapping on my thigh. I pull out my phone and glance at it. The number hasn't been used in two years.

It's my best weapon right now.

Derek clears his throat. "Haley, I'm sorry about the program. But we're going to have to cut it, effective this week."

"No. You're not." I lift my face to the circle of executives.

"Excuse me?"

"I can get him for you." My voice is level even though my stomach turns over.

The head of production scoffs, but Derek leans in.

"A new Riot Act album will get Wicked attention," I go on. "A couple of singles picked up by Hollywood for summer blockbusters. And most importantly, everyone will be calling for interviews. Which means we can get our artists—all of them—back in the spotlight."

Todd laughs. "I heard about your father's track record of finding talent, but what you're talking about isn't magic. It's voodoo. Jax Jamieson's vanished off the face of the earth."

I ignore Todd and turn to Derek. "Two conditions: One, I produce the album. Two, you don't cut my program until after the album's recorded. It goes platinum in the first month, we keep the program."

"You can't be serious," Todd says flatly, but Derek's gaze is fixed on me.

"You think you can make it happen?" he asks.

"Get a studio ready." I hold out a hand. "Do we have a deal?"

He shakes.

I finger the sheet of paper in my jacket

pocket, then I nod to the lawyer. "Call Jax again. Only this time, you're going to tell him this..."

Thank you for reading *Bad Girl*! I hope you enjoyed the continuation of Jax and Haley's story of love, loss and life off tour.

Find out whether the label that broke them apart can bring them back together in **Wicked Girl**...

I appreciate your help in spreading the word, including telling a friend. Reviews help readers find books! Thank you for leaving a review on your favorite book site.

Sign up for Piper Lawson's newsletter to get free books, exclusive deals and more: www.piperlawsonbooks.com/subscribe

---

NEXT UP FOR JAX AND HALEY...

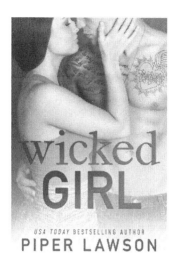

Read a short excerpt below

CHAPTER ONE
Jax

"Jax." Across the table, Camille Taylor's tongue darts out to brush her lip. "We need to talk."

Everything about her reads indecisive, which undermines the professional look she's got going on. High-neck blouse. Bun like a ballerina.

If she wanted to be a ballerina once, this gig must've been a rude awakening.

"What's the problem?" I ask, impatient, shifting in the padded leather chair and eyeing her up over the desk.

"It's Anne. She's been here a year. But she doesn't seem to be settling in."

Annie's eighth grade homeroom teacher flicks her gaze toward the classroom door, like my kid can hear her from the hall.

"She's creative. Smart. But she keeps to herself. I don't think she's making many friends. Occasionally she's disruptive."

My shoulders tighten. "Disruptive how."

She hesitates before uttering a string of words I'm sure I've misheard.

"What?" I demand.

"She glued feminine hygiene products to one of her classmate's books."

Shit.

I fight the urge to rip one of my fingernails. They're all pretty much gone anyway.

"Oh, and Jax?"

"Yeah?"

"Is she channeling that creativity into other outlets? She was telling one of the boys in class about your music."

I shake my head. "She swims. She doesn't even listen to my music."

"I find that hard to believe. We don't know everything our children do."

"Annie doesn't keep secrets from me." My jaw tightens.

"Anne's a bright girl. She's got excellent language and math skills. I wish she'd connect more with the other students—use her abilities more constructively." Her gaze flicks past me, nervous, then back. "I understand from her file she's had some changes recently. That can lead to acting out."

My hands tighten on the armrests. "Tell you what. You do your job and I'll do mine."

I shove out of my chair and cross to the door.

"Annie." Outside, the red head of hair lifts from where she's studying her phone with a pained expression. "Let's go."

We follow the sidewalk out the front of the private school. It's all brick and landscaping, and I wonder again what the money pays for that's so different from the public school I went to. More trees? The lawn gets mowed every week instead of once a month?

I glance over at my kid.

In her school uniform, she looks the same as any other eighth grader in this place. But in the past few years, she's changed.

She wears her hair differently. It used to be in

braids and now it's down or in a ponytail, the kind that sticks out of the top of her head.

I hit the locks on the Bentley, and we both shift inside.

I put the car in gear and pull out of the lot. "Miss Taylor says you glued something to some kid's books."

Caramel eyes land on me for the first time all night. "They're called tampons, Jax."

Her lilting voice wraps around each word like she's underlining them.

It barely registers that she calls me by my first name anymore. I curse whatever god exists that it's my job to ask, "Why?"

"She swiped mine from gym last week. So I figured if she needed them so badly, she could have them."

"When did you get your... you know?"

"Period?" She sighs, shifting in the passenger seat to look out the window. "A few months ago. Don't worry. Mom helped me when I saw her at Christmas."

It takes all my control not to swerve.

It's almost April.

I still haven't done anything about the "you're becoming a woman" literature my manager rustled up for me. It's in a locked drawer, next to the stack of cash I'll use for the hit on the misguided kid who asks her to prom in four years.

Four years? Jesus.

Some days I think that if I'd known the custody battle with Grace for my kid would've taken a year of our lives and dragged my sister through the mud—something she blames entirely on me when I drop my kid off for holiday visits—maybe I wouldn't have done it.

But I can't say that. I can't even let myself think it for long or I find myself reaching for a crutch. Because this is what I wanted. Everything I wanted.

If it's not enough, I don't know what I'll do.

I force myself back to the conversation. "She also said you were talking about my work. My music."

The noise sounds like a snort. "That's not your work anymore. You haven't touched a guitar all year. You used to play with Ryan."

"Uncle Ryan."

"The last time he came by was six months ago."

Christ, she notices everything. It doesn't feel

like that long since I saw Mace, but her mind's like a damn video recorder.

Outside our house, I hit the button on my visor and the gates swing open. The Bentley cruises up the long drive, past the rows of trees and flower beds someone planted a long time ago.

We live fifteen minutes from the school and she doesn't have any friends close by. For the first time, I wonder why not.

"Annie?"

"Anne."

"*Annie.*"

She grinds her teeth next to me. I want to shake her or point out she's living in a damn mansion with everything she could want. And some days, it's as if she doesn't notice.

I take a breath to steady myself as I hit the button for the garage and angle the car inside. "I've never seen you with any friends from school."

"I hang out with Cash and Drew at lunch."

"No girls."

"So?"

"Your teacher thought you might be trying to impress a boy."

She snorts. "Those two are not worth impressing."

"Good." Relief has my shoulders sagging, because if she's into boys, I can't deal with that.

"Do you want to know if I'm a lesbian?"

How I manage to throw the car into park, I'll never know. Especially when every instinct is to hit reverse and mash on the gas pedal of life.

"You're thirteen years old."

"I'll be fourteen in the summer." She opens her door and scrambles out, leaning back in after. "If I do like boys, I wouldn't waste my time on either of them. Drew is smashing Chloe Hastings, and I'm pretty sure Cash doesn't have testicles."

The door slams before I can process those words.

I rub my fingers over the bridge of my nose. There's no way this week could get worse.

Until my phone rings.

End of Sample

To continue reading, be sure to pick up *Wicked Girl* at your favorite retailer.

BOOKS BY PIPER LAWSON

FOR A FULL LIST PLEASE GO TO
PIPERLAWSONBOOKS.COM/BOOKS

OFF-LIMITS SERIES

Turns out the beautiful man from the club is my new professor... But he wasn't when he kissed me.

Off-Limits is a forbidden age gap college romance series. Find out what happens when the beautiful man from the club is Olivia's hot new professor.

WICKED SERIES

Rockstars don't chase college students. But Jax Jamieson never followed the rules.

Wicked is a new adult rock star series full of nerdy girls, hot rock stars, pet skunks, and ensemble casts you'll want to be friends with forever.

RIVALS SERIES

At seventeen, I offered Tyler Adams my home, my life, my heart. He stole them all.

Rivals is an angsty new adult series. Fans of forbidden romance, enemies to lovers, friends to lovers, and rock star romance will love these books.

ENEMIES SERIES

I sold my soul to a man I hate. Now, he owns me.

Enemies is an enthralling, explosive romance about an American DJ and a British billionaire. If you like wealthy, royal alpha males, enemies to lovers, travel or sexy romance, this series is for you!

TRAVESTY SERIES

My best friend's brother grew up. Hot.

Travesty is a steamy romance series following best friends who start a fashion label from NYC to LA. It contains best friends brother, second chances, enemies to lovers, opposites attract and friends to lovers stories. If you like sexy, sassy romances, you'll love this series.

PLAY SERIES

I know what I want. It's not Max Donovan. To hell with his money, his gaming empire, and his joystick.

Play is an addictive series of standalone romances with slow burn tension, delicious banter, office romance and unforgettable characters. If you like smart, quirky, steamy enemies-to-lovers, contemporary romance, you'll love Play.

MODERN ROMANCE SERIES

When your rich, handsome best friend asks you to be his fake girlfriend? Say no.

Modern Romance is a smart, sexy series of contemporary romances following a set of female friends running a relationship marketing company in NYC. If you enjoy hot guys who treat their families like gold, fun antics, dirty talk, real characters, steamy scenes, badass heroines and smart banter, you'll love the Modern Romance series.

ABOUT THE AUTHOR

Piper Lawson is a WSJ and USA Today bestselling author of smart and steamy romance.

She writes women who follow their dreams, best friends who know your dirty secrets and love you anyway, and complex heroes you'll fall hard for.

Piper lives in Canada with her tall and brilliant husband. She's a sucker for dark eyes, dark coffee, and dark chocolate.

For a complete reading list, visit
www.piperlawsonbooks.com/books

Subscribe to Piper's VIP email list
www.piperlawsonbooks.com/subscribe

amazon.com/author/piperlawson

bookbub.com/authors/piper-lawson

instagram.com/piperlawsonbooks

facebook.com/piperlawsonbooks

goodreads.com/piperlawson

THANK YOUS

This book wouldn't have happened without the support of my awesome advance team and reader group (ladies - thank you for the support, nail biting, and patiently rocking in the corner while I finished part 3). Pam and Renate, thank you for your eagle eyes! Nothing gets by you. Mandee, thank you for creating Jax's rock star-worthy signature, Jax is at least 20% more badass now. Natasha, you are the most amazing designer, thank you for letting me tweak this until we got it just right. Lindee, I couldn't imagine better photography to inspire my books. Cassie and Devon, thank you for questioning, polishing, and pointing out I meant to say IV chord, not iV chord. Danielle, thank you for the amazing promo graphics, and generally helping me stay organized and making sure I don't release new books in a vacuum. Plus of course Mr. L, the world's best beta reader and the guy who makes sure my world doesn't break while I'm sequestered in my writing cave. Thank you all from the bottom of my heart.